it's about time

it's about time

Lara Crissey

This is a work of fiction. Names, characters, places and incidents either
are the product of the author's imagination or are used fictitiously, and any
resemblance to any actual persons, living or dead, events, or locales is
entirely coincidental.

This book was printed in the United States of America.

To order additional copies of this book, contact:
Xlibris Corporation
1-888-795-4274
www.Xlibris.com
Orders@Xlibris.com
95367

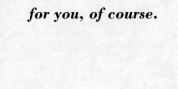

for you, of course.

Acknowledgements

First and foremost, thank you to all of my friends for your love and support, encouragement and enthusiasm. As anyone reading this will know, it truly is about time! "Claire" has been sitting around in various iterations for a few years now. I've been asked many times, "How's Claire?" or "Where's Claire?"—sometimes jokingly, sometimes not. The timing has never been right to finish this story . . . until now. And I can't tell you why, other than to say that, simply, it's time.

Special thanks to the friends who very clearly shaped some of my characters. Danielle, Ann, Lyndsay, Alex . . . Bob Kimer . . . you know who you are. I adore the people in my life and feel immensely grateful every day for the kindness, honesty, communication, and fun shared. As someone who rarely uses the word never, I can say this: I never take any of you for granted.

It's About Time is fiction, but parts of it are based on some of my experiences. For those of you who've been there during the times I recount, you may laugh or feel sadness in recollection. Just know that I am grateful I didn't go through these times alone.

Obviously, my theme of time is constant. (Get it?) For years, I created self-imposed deadlines, unrealistic expectations, I focused on time and what I needed to get done . . . instead of focusing on my life, and what I wanted to do. What would make me happy. Fulfilled. Genuinely me. I put my watch away and focused on quality time.

I believe in my heart that timing is critical. We're ready to accept things more readily when we have perspective. And when we realize that we can let go, be vulnerable, be authentic, take risks . . . and we'll still be ok . . . well, there's a lightness in that feeling that cannot be described with words.

When I finally finished my story on a rainy Sunday afternoon, I was listening to music. I know, shocking. Anyone who knows me understands that music is a large part of my life. The song was Ryan Adams' "This Is It." The words made me stop and smile. I would have called it coincidental, but I knew better. It was a gift being handed to me. And a gift is special, no matter when you receive it . . .

Chapter 1

Margery was thinking about the fact that she was hungry. Did I eat this morning, she wondered. *I got up and made the kids breakfast, took out the garbage, helped Sean with his science project, cleaned Kitty's litter box and then Bob needed me to get that key made, and no, I have not eaten anything today.* She had decided to get a pedicure while she was out and had neglected to feed herself. Damn, she thought, as her stomach growled. She stared at the girl sitting almost directly in front of her, getting her nails done. She thought, That girl's hair is the color of pure milk chocolate. I need to get a candy bar as soon as I leave here.

In her head, Claire-with-the-chocolate-brown-hair developed her to do list for the weekend as she sat and had her nails done. She looked mindlessly at the women (and one man) getting pedicures, and considered why people would go to such lengths to make their feet pretty. And then she starting thinking of feet in general and shook her head in disgust. In her mind she thought, Gross Claire, why do you do that? Go to gross places and take me along for the ride. What is it that makes you unable to turn your eyes away from the grotesque?

So that to-do list, she reminded herself, back to that to-do list.

Groceries
Clean
Gym
Manicure (cool, I can check that off, once my nails are dry, she thought)
Baby gift for Kate
Cook for the week
Pick up prescription

And midway through her list, she thought of her best friend Alex, who had said to her days before: I think you need some more fun in your life. I have fun, Claire had protested, but then she sat and watched her nails get their final coat of "wicked" and realized maybe she wasn't having all that much fun. Maybe she was too regimented. Maybe it's how she protected herself.

Wait though, she was online and dating and getting to know people. She was going to the gym and spinning and spending time with wonderful friends and going rock climbing (so what if it was indoors) and she learning how to snowboard and she was . . . she was so good at talking herself into things.

Claire had always thought of herself as average. Average height, average weight, average looks. And yet, people would tell her she had beautiful eyes. She had happily accepted her blue eyes, unlike others who complained about their eye color, as if that's worth spending any energy on. There was a kindness in her eyes that was undeniable and obvious to everyone . . . everyone that paid attention anyway. Dark brown, wavy hair that spanned down to the middle of her back. A complexion like milk, creamy and clean, and she probably thought that was the best of her physical atrributes. She disliked her ankles and had a weird fixation on them. She noticed them whenever she worked out in short pants. She worked out a lot but her body seemed to always stay the same. Her friends told her that it was because she looked fine the way she was, but she always knew she could look better, she just wasn't sure how, unless she developed an eating disorder. A perpetual size 6, she knew she looked "fine" but strived for bigger things. Like a smaller body. But then, she also knew she thought too much about it. Nothing shocking there though, because Claire seemed to exist to think and analyze.

Chapter 2

Claire sat at her desk, feeling drained and tired. She decided to call Alex. Alex would understand, she thought, even if she does have to listen to the minutiae of my life. That's what friends are for, right?

Hey Alex, it's Claire.

Claire, what's going on, you sound exhausted.

I had another dream again about Douglas last night.

Oh man, again?

I know. It must be the weather or something.

What? That doesn't even make sense.

Oh well, sometimes nothing makes sense. I can't figure it out. I dream of him, every day for a week, and then not at all for months. He's just somehow still in the back of my mind and—

But Claire, it's been what, like 18 years?

I know.

Have you ever thought of trying to find him? Remember when we sat in your apartment and you googled Ryan for me and you called and got his mom and—

I remember. I'm not googling Douglas. He's the one who walked away. I need to come to terms with that.

Maybe you need to find him and ask him what happened.

I know what happened. I was there. He wasn't. I have to go, teleconference in three minutes.

Lucky you.

I'll email you later, k?

You got it sister.

Love you.

Love you too.

I do love my friends, Claire thought. I am lucky. I mean, I am fortunate. Who cares about the past? Why can't we just leave it there, she thought? And then she immediately took it back. For all the sad memories, there were amazing, glorious memories that she would cry to part with. No, it's worth the pain to have the joy. It reminded her of Kahlil Gibran. What did he say? You can only know joy when you have known sadness, and you can only know sadness when you have known joy.

OK, Claire, back to reality. You need to get on this conference call. Time to discuss transient ischemic strokes and the value of grassroots initiatives with your marketing colleagues. Claire was also grateful for her job. She enjoyed what she did for a living and felt very fortunate that she had found something meaningful that involved writing and dealing with health issues. Having been in and out of hospitals as a kid for her asthma, watching her best friend in high school battle depression, and growing up with alcoholic parents, she felt an important tie to healthcare and knew that it was the place for her to be. Public relations meant a good deal of writing, which was her favorite pastime aside from reading, taking pictures, and baking. She usually made it a point to bake when she had dreams about Douglas. It distracted her mind in an amazing way. The problem was, Alex was starting to catch on to her pattern. The day she brought her crème puffs, Alex sighed and said, Oh Claire, another Douglas dream? This one must have been good; these things look delicious.

Chapter 3

We are standing on the dock in Newport News. It's a bright, beautiful sunny day. I'm looking at you and the sun is in my eyes. It makes me squint. I want to change the angle of where we are standing, so that I can see you without squinting. But I don't want to move. I want to remember how you are looking at me this very moment, you in your torn, worn jeans, your baseball shirt with navy blue sleeves, that big bright smile making every inch of me warm. I want your arms around me, but then I won't see your face.

People look at us and smile. How can they not? We are totally, completely, hopelessly in love. First time for both of us. I think we must look like we are floating.

You are talking but I can't really hear you. I can hear Bono singing "All I Want is You." I want to cry, it is so beautiful and perfect. You seem to be telling me that you love me and you don't want to leave, but you have to. In front of my eyes, you change from the current Douglas—the only Douglas I know—to a future Douglas. And suddenly you are no longer in front of me, but in front of a bunch of kids who you appear to be coaching for some sort of little league game. I'm yelling to you. Douglas! Douglas! Where did you go? Why aren't you here with me? And you look up, as if you hear something, but it's just the clink of a bat that has caught your attention, and now I am so far away from you that you've become out of focus. I think I am still yelling for you but I have no voice. I'm trying, but nothing is coming out.

Chapter 4

Claire had awoke in a sweat saying "Douglas." It was 2:41 in the morning. She had a drink of water and lied on her back, staring at the ceiling. What the hell, she thought. 18 flippin years and I am still having these dreams. I will not look him up though. He left and he had a reason. Some things are just better left undone. It's all in the rear view, she said out loud. Someone at work had said that to her once and she liked the way it sounded. So complete. If time is really one continuum, then that sentence makes sense. But is time really one continuum? Not if she believed Richard Bach or Deepak Chopra or Albert Einstein. She shook her head. You will never get back to sleep if you start thinking of time and the universe and all that crap, she warned herself. She flipped on the light and reached over for her current book, The Double by Jose Saramago. This is one amazing author, she thought. I wish I could write like this.

Chapter 5

It was raining when Claire woke up, and she had to drag herself out of bed. It was going to be a long day. Meetings in the morning, a presentation to her boss in the afternoon and then therapy after work. Sometimes she liked that and sometimes she didn't. She dreaded the days that she had dreamt of Douglas because they would analyze the crap out of it. Moreover, they would analyze the way that that relationship had affected all of her relationships afterwards. The choices she had made, the trust issues she developed, which she argued were already there before Douglas, the desire she had to be close to someone, and her therapist's insistence that she really didn't want to be close to anyone except her friends—she'd had opportunities and managed to either sabotage them or just walk away. She hated hearing that, because on some level, she knew it was true. But she also knew that she had gotten involved with some cold people because she knew what to expect from both them and from herself. If I'm with someone like this, I won't be disappointed. I'll know that they don't have the capacity to love me, so I won't really be hurt or surprised when it comes to an end. Ugh, she didn't like confessing to understanding all of this. But the truth was her ultimate goal, finding truth inside herself and finding it in someone else. She was ready. At least, she thought she was. And wasn't that what mattered?

Chapter 6

I'm tired of talking about Douglas, Claire said to Dr. Blake. Patty Blake, PhD. A thin, blonde woman, petite, with perfectly tailored little suits that fit her as if she were a Barbie doll. Like they were made for her. Claire envied her, with degrees from Cornell and Columbia hanging on the wall, her handsome boyfriend with the big choppers, whose picture sat on her desk, along with the dog, an American Indian Husky named Chief. Other pictures included: Patty finishing the Boston Marathon (looking cute and pulled together despite the 26.2 miles she had just run), Patty with her parents on one of her many graduation days, Patty with her 3 brothers playing football on Thanksgiving, with a smile as wide as humanly possible, so genuine it was heartbreaking. Sometimes Claire would think: I wish I was you, Patty Blake.

Patty was talking about trusting your gut and listening to your instincts, a recurrent theme in their discussions. She reminded Claire about things she had said about her ex-husband.

Claire, you've told me on more than one occasion that Rick alienated you from early on in your relationship, that he never treated you as an equal, and that he told you right away that you would never come first in his life.

Claire nodded, and her stomach twisted into the familiar comfortable knot that it knew so well. Suck it up, she thought, that which does not kill me makes me stronger, she thought, you are doing this to get to a better place, she reminded herself.

Why did you accept that, Patty Blake was asking. But before Claire could respond, Patty said, I think we need to talk about the relationship you had with your father, and at that, Claire's stomach-knot did a somersault that caused her to touch her belly and let an audible heavy sigh escape her lips. Patty smiled in a way that was kind and understanding and it made Claire's heart swell. She felt like she should get into all of that just because Patty was so nice. But the double-knot in her stomach said "why bother, Claire?"

She took a deep breath and said "Ok, Dr. Blake, we can talk about Mike."

Mike Cassidy was a genius, or so Claire deduced. He had to be, he was her dad. And he was always reading some big, thick book that sounded really deep. But from a young age, she saw this genius get stoned every day and lose touch with reality on too many occasions to count. His smell was a mix of cigarettes, pot, beer and coffee. It seemed like his constant scent. As she remembered it, she thought of Pigpen from Charlie Brown, and how he walked around in a cloud of dust. That was Mike. Only he walked around in a haze of pot and cigarette smoke, which clouded his emotions but not his intellect. He was an emotionally damaged person, which made him a complex and unfortunately rather demented father.

On second thought, Dr. Blake, would it be ok if we waited until later? I actually dreamt of Douglas again last night and think maybe I need to do that exercise we talked about . . . you know, that whole "unsent letter" business you keep going on about.

Patty looked a little hurt, and Claire immediately regretted the way she had phrased it. I'm sorry, Dr. Blake, she said, I didn't mean it like that. I just meant that I think I like that idea.

Dr. Blake brushed it off, wanting to keep Claire to her word on this. Claire, she said, this isn't going to be easy, but I'm glad you feel ready to acknowledge some of this. I think it will be really helpful for you.

And so, having been given some rather specific guidelines, Claire went home with a brand new purple spiral notebook from Target . . . and a rather pricy bottle of Chianti. "Because I'm worth it" she mimicked the Loreal commercial and chuckled. It was more to hide the fear than anything. Humor was such a great way to mask fear.

*   *   *

Later that night, Claire sat down on her bed with her favorite Stabilo pen and her new notebook, not knowing where to begin.

Dear Douglas,

I'm not really sure where to begin. This feels weird and awkward. Let me tell you what I'm doing. I'm 36 years old and I am writing to you, the man—the young man—I fell in love with 19 years ago, when I was just 17, because although you walked out of my life, you never really left my heart. I'm trying to get you out of it so I can move on. Not so eloquently put, but you get the idea.

When we met, you were beautiful and perfect to me. You had a lovely southern accent and you told me all about Texas, and how it really was the best state in this country. You believed that, and that made it ok for you to say. I met you because my sister and my brother-in-law decided to meddle in my life. I was young and confused and uneasy and went down to visit them in Virginia. You changed shifts with Michael the night that I arrived in town so that he could go with Amanda to pick me up. And in turn, he said "you can meet my sister-in-law." As if that was some sort of prize. I was annoyed, because I'm not ashamed to admit it now—at the time, I was a little angry about life in general. I wonder sometimes how you remember me, because while I am fundamentally the same person, I feel like I am in such a better, more positive place. For the most part. I think I was bitter towards my dad way back then. I'm not anymore. I'm not bitter at all. Just sometimes . . . I am really just surprised at how my life panned out.

I cannot seem to get past the fact that you loved me one day intensely and sincerely, and then the next day you were gone without a trace. I had no way of knowing anything, just that you had abruptly ended your lease, paying some crazy penalties. Your home was cleared out as though done by the grinch himself. You donated your car to charity and unbelievably, you had brought Smoky to the animal shelter the day before. Years back, I kept going over and over the timing of these events. I hadn't been at your apartment that day, but I remember giving you treats for Smoky, and you were psyched, because he liked those Snausages you said, and you said you would be sure to say that they were a gift from me. I loved that dog. Did you know that I went to the shelter and found him, and brought him home? At first I thought all of it was some weird creepy big mistake. It wasn't a bad dream, but I did feel like I was in a daze and watching myself somehow from above, and everything was happening to me in the third person. I only went to the shelter because that's where we picked him out. I was stunned to see him there. It meant to me that you really wanted to be alone. No Claire, no Smoky, no friends. I never knew your family, so there was no way to reach them. We were all baffled and for a lot of sleepless nights I pictured scenarios from horror movies or America's Most Wanted episodes.

The police wouldn't talk to me. They said it was a matter that they would not discuss with anyone but your immediate family, and you had no one here so that was that. Even the media, they never even covered the story about the guy that poof! was one day here, the next day gone. But then I spoke with a couple of sympathetic sociologists and such and they said that the pattern and methodology you had employed pointed to you wanting to leave a situation practically "without a trace." Those words always lingered with me, so you can imagine how I hated when a few years ago that show "Without a Trace" came on TV.

I don't know why, but I knew you weren't dead. In time, I found myself assuming that nothing bad had happened to you. But I don't know for sure. So I worried for years. I was scared to get involved in relationships. To get close to anyone, really. My whole mindset of "everyone important in my life has abandoned me" was further validated when you left "without a trace." I couldn't understand why you would do something like that to me. You certainly must not have loved me, was what I figured.

That day that we met, do you remember? I do, it's clear like it was yesterday. Like it was this morning even. You walked to the car with Michael, your smile as bright as the sun in the sky. You wore those super-faded jeans with the rip in the knee, they looked so cool and authentic to me and they were so 80s. You wore a red long sleeve baseball shirt from the Gap and as you approached the car I remember saying to my sister, "Oh my God." I thought you were the most beautiful boy I had ever seen. I tried so hard to be cool when you got in the car, my insides were fluttering out of control and I felt like I needed to sit on my hands; they were squirmy and overly-expressive. You had the grayest eyes, I noticed, as you leaned in to say hello, but they were surprisingly warm and inviting. I had never been a big fan of gray eyes, I thought they looked, in general, cold and distant. Maybe it was the whole package. You were 20 and already had a lot of gray hair. You looked young and yet distinguished at the same time, and I just wanted to instantly be close to you. I wanted you to know me and I wanted to know you.

We talked about music. You were obsessed with Adam Ant! It was funny, as I think back on it. All that goofy techno sounding music that we took so seriously. We were young and we only had the music of the times. We both loved it and that first night we listened to your new INXS **cassette.** *The one with "Never Tear Us Apart" which became, ironically, our theme song. We had spent the whole day together, me, you, Amanda and Michael, and I had not smiled consistently for a whole day in a long time. Spending time with you melted away any tension and uneasiness I had. I was myself and you were you and we laughed and went bowling and ate pizza and oh yeah . . . we drank too much. Do you remember, I tried to keep up with you and Michael drinking Jaegermeister? That was stupid. But once I barfed I was fine. I remember laying on the bed with my sister, while you and Michael spoke loudly (was it that you were speaking loudly because you were drunk, or did it just sound loud to me because I was drunk? Funny that I still wonder about that). I said to Amanda in a dreamy and tipsy way, Douglas is amazing. I said it more to the air and the universe, but since she was there, it was like I was telling her.*

Wow, I have totally digressed. I know I'm going to have a hard time sleeping tonight for sure. But I am committed to doing this. Douglas, you were the love of my life. The first person ever in my life who felt honest and true and real and solid. When you held me in your arms, I actually felt safe, as though no one could hurt me. No one could reach me. As though you were some magic shield. A magnetic field. We were the only ones there. We were the only people that mattered. It felt that way. It's so lovely to remember.

It was like that for a while. I was still in school while you were working for the government down in Virginia. I would take the train for ten hours on Fridays to come and see you, and Mondays I would return. Good thing my mom didn't give a rat's ass about school. She would periodically give me half-ripped pages from my notebooks that said : sincerely, Jackie Cassidy. That was it. I was able to fill in the rest. Insert ailment here. Claire was out yesterday because of her asthma. Claire was out yesterday because she has a bad cold. Claire was out sick last week because she can't cope with her mom being in rehab and living alone.

You would pick me up at the train station and my legs would be like jello from sitting for hours and then they would feel like jello because I was excited to see you. I loved knowing that there was only one stop left before I was going to see you, that shiny happy gorgeous face, smiling at ME and no one else, just me. Could I have ever felt more special? It was crazy and amazing. I loved every bit of it. It feels so goofy to say now, but I really would fall into your arms upon exiting the train and we would kiss as though we were long lost lovers (irony again). We couldn't get close enough to each other and we always had to be touching in some capacity, whether it was holding hands or squeezing our legs together or kissing or me touching your knee through the whole in your jeans, or God, the way you played with my hair, it made me want to cry and want to rip your clothes off at the same time.

Speaking of . . . that first time for us, do you remember? Uh oh. I think I'm supposed to share this letter with my therapist. Oh, who cares, I'm on a roll and I don't want to stop. Something I have learned is that I don't want to limit myself in how I express myself and share my feelings. I've learned some harsh lessons as a result. (Some people actually do like to live in a bubble and not hear authentic feelings.) Heck, I can't judge. I know I was like that when I was younger too. I actually think I should credit you for breaking through my hard exterior. In fact, it wasn't all that hard, was it? It was like an eggshell really. Delicate.

I borrowed one of Amanda's "sexy" lingeries. I chose black and lacy. She had a lot to choose from, and she and I tried to laugh off the weirdness that my big sister was sharing her intimate apparel with me so that I could have sex for the first time. I remember thinking "ew, my sister got down in these clothes." And yet. I was INSANELY nervous and couldn't really eat my pizza that night. I remember sitting across from you at Pizza Hut wondering if you really wanted to be with me. You'll remember I didn't have such a stellar self-esteem. But there you were, looking at me with kind and loving eyes and I knew I would somehow make it through this night. I didn't, however, think that I would be writing to you about it 18 years later. I thought for sure we would be talking about it on our front porch for the rest of our lives. I would say things like, "remember when you stopped kissing me and went underneath the sheets and I couldn't understand why you were going down there?" And we would laugh and I would inevitably snort and you would remind me how I had such a hard time relaxing and kept my legs so tight. We would have both laughed that night, as we fumbled around on that aqua couch that Amanda and Michael bought at Seaman's (again with the irony), had we not both been so nervous. Ok, ok, yes, me more so than you. Fine.

When I walked into the living room, it was aglow from Amanda's blue lava lamp, which was a recent Christmas present from Michael. I must admit, it was the perfect mood lighting. Who needs candles when you have a lava lamp? I sat down on the edge of the couch, it was a futon-ish thing that pulled out into the size of a double bed. Remember? It was very retro. Anyway. I had that big flippin robe on and underneath, the lingerie that wasn't mine. Awkward. You told me to "get into bed" and I sheepishly took off the robe. When I got in next to you, you said, I don't really like those things. Take it off. My heart sank. It wasn't the best way to boost my confidence. But soon after I removed Amanda's lacy clothes, you were close by my side, kissing me slowly and deeply, and I thought for sure that life would be fine if that never stopped.

Claire wrote two additional pages detailing their first night together, and sighed heavily. Her last sentences were, *I don't think of that night too much. But as you can see, I remember it vividly. And I'm glad I do.* But then she struck all of the detail, feeling foolish, feeling exposed, and feeling a little warm as well. She decided to re-write the letter without the sudden burst of sexual energy, and picked up with:

Ours was the first major relationship in my life, and I wanted so badly to be perfect for you. I wanted to be just what you wanted. If I could have read your mind and learned what you considered "perfect", I would have given up any semblance of myself to emulate the image you wanted. Not healthy. I just wanted you to always love me. I've given up on always's and never's these days. Too definitive for me. The past, present and future blend together and I've learned that always and never don't ALWAYS live up to their promises. That's ok.

I'm writing this letter to you which I will not send to ask why you left without a trace, why you never told me where you were going, why you never said goodbye, why you put Smoky in a shelter, why I never felt you kiss me again, why you never made those designs on my legs again. You used to quiz me, remember? What was that? A smiley face? A heart? The letter C? I could never get enough of that. Huh, I said never...quite a few times.

Chapter 7

Claire met Alex at Café Atlantique after work. Well, technically after working out. It was 7pm and already dark, which left Claire feeling sluggish and out of sorts. She hated when they had to set the clocks back or forward, and for the week following, she would take every opportunity to tell herself and anyone else that the *real* time was x.

They sat down with their glasses of Chianti and waited for their salads.

So I started writing to Douglas, Claire announced. I'm afraid it sounds more like I'm trying to write erotica than try to figure out why my boyfriend disappeared from my life though.

Right on, said Alex. A little erotica never hurt anyone.

I think it has something to do with the fact that I haven't been intimate with anyone in a long time, Claire analyzed.

Whatever Claire, you have lots of opportunities, it's your whole mental/physical wanting-to-have-a-connection thing that stops you. You know you could get laid if you wanted to.

Get laid, Claire repeated. How romantic, Alex.

I'm just saying, she said, and went to retrieve their salads.

Over dinner, they discussed the merits of the Unsent Letter. Alex thought it was bullshit, look the guy up and confront him, fuck that shit of pouring out your emotions in a freakin letter, just be done with it, find him, call him, drive to his home, fly across the country if you have to, just find out what the hell happened and move on with your life.

Claire doubted that this event—Douglas' mysterious and abrupt departure—had been the catalyst for all of her miserable (wait, that's too harsh she thought) relationships. She did think that it made her doubt herself and her self-worth and it did influence how she would feel in all future intimate relationships. She was remembering the letter she had written to him when he first left, the original unsent letter, the one in which she said she would never love anyone again and would never let anyone get close to her again. She laughed at her foolish and dramatic statements as a young woman.

Alex was saying "um, hello, earth to Claire" and Claire said, You know, let's not talk about this anymore. I'm writing a letter to Douglas, it isn't finished because well, for one, I was getting all torqued, and for another, it was getting too long and I needed a break. I was getting too detailed and was losing my train of thought.

Shocking! said Alex, with unapologetic sarcasm. They laughed like kids and gulped their wine like juice.

Chapter 8

Alex was Claire's best friend. And yet, they were different in a lot of ways. Claire was an introvert; Alex, an extrovert. When Alex walked into a room, she commanded attention just by being there. A wide, warm smile, hellos to friends and strangers, hugs, kisses, she had it down. You could say that she knew how to work a room, but it wouldn't be exactly accurate. Because she wasn't working the room—she was being genuine.

Claire could be tentative about a lot of things—Alex was not. Alex would say what she wanted, when and why. Sometimes Claire was jealous of that. But they seemed to balance each other. There were times when guys would ask if they were girlfriends—half seriously, half just imagining a pillow fight gigglefest. They were close. They both had tumultuous childhoods, they both married men older than them with kids, they both divorced these men, and they both had picked up their lives more times than they cared to think about.

Claire and Alex met in the small community gym where they lived. Alex was new, Claire had been there post-divorce for about a year. At the time, Claire kept to herself, getting up early, going to work before security had the chance to turn on the lights, going home and working out until she couldn't see straight, and then taking a shower, making a salad, and reading. To say she was regimented would be a gross understatement.

It all changed—slowly—when she met Alex.

Alex was younger than Claire, 28, full of energy and life and just glowing with potential. They chatted on the treadmills and exchanged numbers and Claire thought "neat, a local friend outside of work" since most of her "friends" were colleagues. She had given up some friends from the marriage and she had, by obvious default, given up her husband's family, which was the core of her social life for 7 years.

Four years later, Alex and Claire were the closest of friends, missing each other when they didn't have a chance to connect on the phone or in person after a day or two. Claire felt in her heart that that's what it felt like to have a sister, and she apologized silently to her real sister, who had almost become a stranger to her.

Chapter 9

Rather than finish her writing to Douglas, Claire figured she would find that letter that she had written so long ago to Rick, her ex-husband—maybe that would help her craft the final piece of the letter to Douglas, she thought. She hadn't been able to shake the lack of closure with Rick, but she recalled that writing the letter had been good for her, and it was always there if she wanted to send it. If she could find it. Always. Ha, she laughed at herself. You said *always*, Claire! She had written the letter pretty fresh out of the relationship, six months or so? she thought to her herself, as she scoured her volumes of journals and dresser drawers. She had almost given up looking when she found it folded neatly within the shiny green journal she had bought when she lived in San Diego. When she opened it up, she saw a post-it note from years ago, which said: My eyes are screaming, and you, deaf to their request, are blind. She laughed at how proud she had been at the time she wrote it: a twenty-year old girl who was very tipsy, at a cool bar in New Haven called The Moon, with her friend Cheryl, who she had to call Dawn, because that was the name on her fake driver's license.

Chapter 10

On the red velvet couch in her apartment, Claire sat clutching her favorite cushion, the brown one with little earth tone flowers she'd purchased at Pier 1. She hesitated slightly before picking up the letter that she had written years ago. Sometimes it felt like another lifetime ago. In fact, thankfully, most times it felt that way.

> *Dear Rick,*
>
> *I really don't want to spend a lot of time on this. I have been spending time thinking about the most effective way to communicate with you. Days, then weeks, have gone by, but I find myself clinging to some fundamental issues that I am now understanding will only be let go in time and with closure. Closure is something I'm not quite sure we accomplished. Perhaps all the lies have clouded my head and therefore I am just not recalling any conversations of finality. Anyway, all that time, I did say that I was willing to talk with you in greater depth. I specifically remember offering to talk more on the day that you said that you can't look at a picture of me without getting a lump in your throat. Question for you: had Kim already moved in at that time?*
>
> *I don't get you Rick, but then, I'm not quite sure I ever did. I told you that I question everything from the 7 years we were together, since there were so many occasions for me to question whether you actually loved me. But if I take a step back, I perhaps can gain a bit of clarity—this may suck to hear but hey, what do I know, maybe you're not even reading this. Maybe you have just thrown it out. So back to me looking at this from an objective point of view—you went from Susan to Kelly to maybe some*

no-names to Tara to me. I am not surprised that from me, you went to someone else (or should I say "during"), followed by yet another woman. In fact, I made a prediction (as you so often did) and shared it with a couple of close friends, even your sister. My prediction was that you would be living with someone within six months. I was therefore completely unfazed by the fact that your new girlfriend had moved in. I was initially embarrassed. Why didn't I pick up on your inability to be alone, when you had been engaged and three months later were asking me out? Why, when I moved in with Kate, did I allow you to bring all of my clothes to your car and in essence move in with you? I guess I don't need to get into the thought processes I have gone through regarding myself as a person, and why I was able to get into a relationship like this. I'll handle that myself.

You gave me reasons to doubt that you loved me all the time, and you also gave me reasons not to trust you. You always put the girls first, and while I truly commend you and respect your excellent relationship with Jane and Leigh, you never quite grasped that you made me feel alone and rejected and unloved. So many times I wished that you had deeper feelings for me. But they just weren't there, and I wish it hadn't taken me so long to figure that out.

There is no doubt in my mind that you cheated on me numerous times in our relationship. If you weren't, there would have been no need to lie. Kerry's phone number, that woman Chris, who called you all the time on your work voicemail, including nights and weekends. Your LAME excuse about listening to voicemails over the weekend: "I just hate seeing that red light on the phone when I get to work." That was so ridiculous. There were more. Weird keys, smells, phone numbers, calls and even strange voicemails at our home, lipstick on your shirt for God's sake! The ultimate cliché which you so casually explained away. Lying was effortless for you. Any of these things and more, you name it. How did I not seek more information? All I did was ask you, and all you did was deny it. Shame on me for not trying harder to find answers. I could have saved us both years of unhappiness. I won't belabor this point. It is what it is.

Indeed, I believe you never had any intention of having a child with me, and perhaps this has been the most emotionally devastating issue to deal with. While certainly the other factors were painful, you do not know and simply cannot imagine the emotional scarring involved in the back and forth conversations about having children. At the time, I could only deduce that you never wanted to have more children, and you knowingly led me through years of indecision, alienating me further, proving that you didn't care about me—all you really cared about was my role as the person who cooked, cleaned, bought gifts, arranged parties, and could be displayed externally as your partner. But you know Rick, we were never partners, because you never saw me as your equal. That, I can almost understand. Fifteen years younger, in a different mindset, a different place in life. But I really conformed to your lifestyle—weekends with the kids, dinner when you got home, dinners with your clients/friends/whatever, family functions. I didn't do much of my own thing. Again, shame on me, I should have put myself first. But I didn't—I put you first. Unfortunately, often I didn't even rank on your list.

But who cares about "lists"? I really intended to be brief, and I think I have been. No closure, that's what has been bugging me. Talking to you and never getting a straightforward answer. Why no straight answers? What did you think I was going to do? Clock you? Hate you? I guess worse: figure you out. You have no idea what it's like to question an entire chunk of your life and to suddenly wonder who the hell you were married to for so long.

We both made mistakes, separately and together. We did everything too quickly. We should not have gotten married so soon, and we should not have had that "secret" wedding. Why did I put that in quotes? It really was a secret. I hated the secret of being married that first year. I couldn't understand why we had to keep it on the down-low, but years later, I get it. You wanted to make sure. You didn't want people to talk. You were calculated, but so smooth and deceptive that at the time, I just felt confused. I was so naïve. At the time I should have taken it as hard evidence that you were unsure of our relationship. If I ever do marry again, I hope my husband-to-be will want to shout to the world that he is in love with me.

It's funny, when I found out about Kim living with you, I was, as I said before, not a bit surprised. After all, this is your pattern. It's a shame that you can't spend some time alone and get to know yourself. Anyway, what upset me—what took my breath away—was that you let her bring her cat. After all those years of bitching about litter boxes and declawing and ruining furniture, fur, ticks, fleas . . . and then someone that you have known for three months moves in along with her cat. That just really hurt.

But no doubt, the final straw was not telling me about Leigh's high school graduation. I was really out of my mind when I spoke with Jane and found out that Leigh's graduation was that night. I was so hurt and angry that I just had to call you. And of course, you had to pretend not to know who it was. And then you whispered "can I call you back?"—that was classic. You hurt my feelings in a deep and profound way when you neglected to tell me about the graduation. I was part of the girls' lives for seven years, and I was always there. I told you numerous times that I wanted to be at the graduation. By not telling me, your actions implied that you didn't give a crap about anything I had ever done for the girls, and that you didn't respect the love that I had for them.

Deduce from this whatever you want. I needed to write it down, get it off my chest. I'm sorry you wasted your time with me, we are definitely two very different people, with different philosophies, values, morals, and different levels of respect. Luckily, the divorce was easy on you, in financial terms. I still have a lawyer telling me I am nuts. It gets old, I just wanted to be fair. And that's not such a bad thing.

I hope that you enjoy your life and I actually hope that one day you find some peace and happiness. Until you come to terms with yourself, that will be difficult. I think I have moved on, and I remember at one time really wanting to be your friend. But a friend is someone who you can trust. I really hope that this letter gives me closure, and perhaps it just takes time. I am taking the time to heal and grow and understand.

If I might just offer a bit of advice: be good and be truthful to whomever you end up with. Make sure you can sometimes put her before others. And give yourself some time, and acknowledge your mistakes, and then forgive yourself. That's what I've tried to do.

—Claire

Chapter 11

Claire set off to meet her friends on a rainy Saturday afternoon at Café Atlantique. It seemed to be the place to meet, most of the time. Within walking distance for most of them. Fun, casual atmosphere. Inviting. An element of honesty and sincerity. Staffed by young bohemian type girls and funky, crazy haired guys. They all wore clothes that only certain people could get away with. Claire often wondered if that's why they were hired. They all looked so cool, and yet, also as if they had just rolled out of bed.

Walking up River Street, she thought of her friends, and how she would have summarized them if they were on Love Connection.

Alex
Age: 33 years old
Marital Status: Divorced
Occupation: sales
She loves her life, has everything to offer, smiles genuinely at people
Favorite drink: Chianti

Danielle
Age: 38 years old
Marital Status: Married, 3 kids
Occupation: Marketing Director
The most successful woman I know
Favorite drink: Champagne

Susan
Age: 30 years old
Marital Status: Never Been Married

Occupation: Teacher
Other: Has been on Match for a while, but doesn't date too frequently
Favorite drink: Rum and Coke

Isabelle
Age: 29 years old
Marital Status: Never Been Married
Occupation: Healthcare sales
A workout maniac, probably less than 10% body fat, gorgeous, and painfully insecure
Favorite drink: Water

Lyndsay
Age: 28 years old
Marital Status: Engaged
Occupation: pastry chef
Learning to golf, used to be in public relations, the sweetest person alive
Favorite drink: Riesling

She laughed at herself because she was interrupted with thoughts of Chuck Woolery's hair.

Chapter 12

So here they were, talking about work (or, complaining about work may be more accurate to say) and of course the subject inevitably turned, as it most often did, to the dating scene. Lindsay was engaged to Billy and Claire thought her to be one of the happiest people she had ever met. Susan and Isabelle and Alex and Claire—all had been dating intermittently. Claire found it draining and kind of depressing, for the most part. Alex had a blast and always had an amusing story. She was of the mindset that she was out meeting people and she was bound to meet some weirdos but she was also going to meet some fun people too. Claire admired her free spirit. Susan hated to date and it didn't seem that she had gotten over her ex-boyfriend yet, the one with the drinking problem, who she had done everything she could for, and he just continued to drink and waste away in a shell of what he used to be, his skin showing signs that his liver was obviously giving up on him. It made Claire's heart heavy. Isabelle rounded out the table. Isabelle was stunningly gorgeous and had no idea. She worked out for about two hours a day and had the best body Claire had ever seen. She envied her and was jealous many times but simply couldn't dislike her because she was so honest and genuine. It was how everyone felt about Isabelle. Secretly (or not so secretly) they all wanted to be her.

As Claire was daydreaming about having ripped abs like Isabelle, she heard Alex say something that sounded like "and his nose was running!"—Claire, tell the story! And so Claire laughed, rolled her eyes and said, Yeah ok everyone, are you ready for the last bizarro date I had? And yet she felt instantly deflated that she had so many weirdos to choose from. After having been *viewed* on Match.com over 6500 times, she still hadn't met anyone that would remotely meet her qualifications: genuine, honest, relatively attractive, amazing sense of humor, sweet, kind, remotely interested in quantum physics . . . and did she mention honest? Instead she got a bunch of freaks. Hmm.

She cleared her throat among the chatter of the women in the corner of the coffee shop. It was warm and she took off her red corduroy jacket. Maybe it was the wine, she was thinking, rather than the actual temperature in here. Ok, everyone, I'm going to tell you about my date with Dave. It was painful. But I love you guys and hopefully this will be fun and we can laugh it off, because when it happened I was pretty much beside myself.

Dave emailed me when I was just about ready to go to visit my family in Ireland. We emailed back and forth a few times and then I went to Ireland and we lost touch.

I hate that, Susan interjected.

Almost 2 months later, he "winked" at me. Do you know what that means? It's the lazy way of saying "hi" on Match. You wink instead of sending an email. It means you are interested in the person without spending the time or energy to say hello, or anything else for that matter. It's weak. Timid. And yet . . . I decided to say hello again. What's the harm?

There was a collective sigh, that it was obviously a mistake. Here's what happened, Claire said, sighing herself:

We spoke a few times. The times we spoke, he asked me all about my intimate details. Why are you divorced? What happened? Are you happy now? How long into your marriage did you decide that you were unhappy? Do you like your job? Do you like your life? Your friends? Are you close to your family? Is your life meaningful?

Wow, I was blown away. He was assertive but in a kind way. He seemed sweet, smart, attentive. Genuine. He wanted to know me, he wanted to understand me and what was important to me. We spoke for an hour that first night. An hour the following night. And the following night. And we made plans to get together the following night: a Saturday. He called me at 8:45, YES I said 8:45 on Saturday morning—which was sort of a red flag for me, but—do you know what he said? He said, "do you know what's so cool about today?" and I asked "what?" and he replied "today I get to meet you!" and I thought that was so simple and sweet that I felt compelled to email him later that day my favorite poem, A Ritual To Read to Each Other. And I thought wow, if only I am attracted to him, he is into the whole physics/universe thing and I can talk with him and we can relate and wow, what if this is the guy, what if this is the guy on the other end of the phone, what are the odds? Still, I felt a little out of sorts that he called me at 8:45 on a Saturday morning. What's up with that? At least say "I know it's early but I had to call you, I just couldn't stand it" but no, it was just like a "hey what's up" very ordinary as if we always spoke on a Saturday morning kind of thing. And so, I realized a breaking line inside of me. This guy might be just a tad weird.

We spoke again that afternoon, he was going to look at real estate and INVITED ME. I thought that was REALLY WEIRD. And yet still, I sat there and thought, ok, I'll meet the guy tonight and see what happens.

At this point Alex interjects, I'm sorry, I would have said "see ya later" if some asshole stranger called me at 8:45 on a Saturday morning.

With this, the group giggles and backs Alex.

Really Claire, what the hell is that all about, asked Lindsay.

Well, Claire sounded apologetic. I just was trying to put myself out there and be positive and open to the possibility.

Another collective sigh resonated in the small side room of the cafe. Everyone was thinking "poor Claire"—even Claire herself.

Well, Claire continued, somewhat despondently, let me finish the story . . .

Everyone laughed and agreed, pushing her to share the rest of the details, because they knew that they were going to be bad, which meant it was going to be good, something to laugh at and something to say "wow, that's worse than my last date was!"

Dave and I met here, because, as everyone knows, this is my safe haven. But I saw him get out of his car and for a split second I almost just kept driving. I wanted to, I really wanted to not spend time with him as soon as I saw him. I know that's awful.

This time everyone moaned and rolled their eyes and said things like "Claire, you're too nice" and "What did he look like?" and there was laughing and drinking of wine and a nice camaraderie of warm friends. Claire felt light and started to get giggly.

Well, for one, I have bigger shoulders than him. He was wearing a Dr. Huxtable sweater. An avid cyclist, he probably had about ten percent body fat. I could have twisted him like a pretzel, she said, which was one of her favorite expressions. They all laughed.

And oh yeah, his face was very sunken in—"chiseled" would have been the ultimate euphemism. I ran into someone from our building that night who said "who's the skull" which is mean but—and again, Claire couldn't hear her voice for all the laughing.

Hair? Isabelle asked, laughing.

Minimal, Claire responded. It was like, super short, like I'm basically bald but keep the fuzz . . . just because . . .

Claire explained the worst part of the date, now that everyone was starting to feel tipsy. His nose kept running, and he wasn't doing anything to stop it, she shared. At this point, forget it, everyone laughed so hard that she just had to stop talking. Alex yelled, I KNOW, HOW DISGUSTING IS THAT? More laughter followed.

Oh and one more thing, Claire said, you just need to hear this. More? Was the collective shout from a bunch of now certainly tipsy women Yes, Claire assured, just one more thing. I told him that I have issues running outside because of my asthma, and he told me his mom also had breathing problems. He told me that she had learned a really neat "trick" for breathing better from an EMT. He said and DEMONSTRATED: what you do is, you bear down and grunt, you bear down *as if you are going to have a bowel movement*. That's what he said to me.

The girls around her were shocked, totally grossed out, and hysterical.

Girl, we have to get you off of Match, Alex said.

You just need to be more selective, Claire, said Susan. That's so nasty.

At least he didn't ask you to drive him to Ikea, joked Danielle.

How did you leave it, asked Lindsay.

Claire said, Well, I've been seeing him ever since, of course! No, she had sent him a courteous and kind email the following day, explaining that, as she liked to put it, "chemistry is squishy and nebulous and hard to define" and that she wasn't feeling it with him.

That's fair, the girls agreed.

But, Claire said, he wrote me this obnoxious email back . . . I just so happen to have it with me. Claire heard Alex say, Claire can pull anything out of that handbag, do you need a toothbrush? A candle? A water? Music? It's like the never-ending bag o' wishes. Claire felt compelled to explain that she had the email because she was compiling a bunch of stuff to start writing a little memoir of all these experiences. They all rolled their eyes again, in a loving way. Maybe again in a little way that said they felt bad for her.

She cleared her throat:

> *Hey Claire, Thanks for the note. I simply thought it would be fun to follow through on the "some level of attraction" thing.*

Although as you mentioned the whole chemistry part is a bit nebulous. In all honesty I figured it would be worth pursuing, if for at least to checkout the sexual compatibility. Nice butt, cut cleavage and an excellent mouth. Oh, and some pretty cool intellect . . . which is a total dealbreaker for me (nice to know it's there). Although I suspect exploring that intimacy thing would lend to uncovering some of those crazy "issues" that hold you captive. Darn it! Best of luck! Dave

She had to read it a few times because no one could really quite get it. As soon as she had said "nice butt, cut cleavage and an excellent mouth" for the third time, she laughed so hard that she snorted, stood up, took a bow and said, Ladies, I'm getting another glass of wine. A lightness in her step hid the slight heaviness in her heart.

Chapter 13

Claire went home that night and set her computer on her lap, deciding that now was as good a time as any to start working on that press release about the importance of secondary stroke prevention and the new trial that could hold promise for new treatment strategies. She yawned and as she began to type, she found herself writing nothing that resembled a press release. Instead, she wrote poetry, she didn't even realize she was writing it until she was done, and she couldn't blame it on the wine, it was just something inside of her that needed to get out.

Sadness overwhelms me today
It is a driving force
I can't turn it off
Or push it away
Or paste on a smile
I feel open
Exposed
Vulnerable
Sad
Directionless
Purposeless
Frightened
What is my legacy?
Who will remember me?
Why is that important, anyway?
Where am I going?
I don't want to be an elderly woman
Bitter
Alone

Filled with thoughts
And regret
And too many "what-ifs" to consider
How do I start again
Before it's too late
Or is it already?

Chapter 14

I'm just calling to confirm that we're still meeting this afternoon, Claire said.

Yes, 4pm, right? That sounds great, I'm looking forward to it, Jim replied.

Jim: another dude from Match, Claire thought. He had a really nice profile and had come up as one of her "potential matches"—this crazy auto-generated email that arrived weekly in her inbox. "Yikes" was her comment most of the time. She had only been on for a few months and was not shaking the creepiness of it all any time soon. But this guy seemed neat and direct. Neat, because he said simple things, like "I like coffee and chocolate"; direct because he said things like "I really want to be in a quality relationship." Claire could relate. So she emailed him, and he had responded, and here she was.

It was 4:30 on a Sunday afternoon in September and Claire was standing at Borders, where she was supposed to meet Jim, "reading" a dessert cookbook. Sponge cake, macadamia nut cookies, chocolate torte . . . she would look up between recipes, feigning interest in their details while all the time thinking "wow, I got stood up." She called Alex and told her, and Alex said, call him, God Claire! She was right. What the hell. She went outside to make the call and there he was. He apologized for being late and they got a cup of coffee. They sat outside and enjoyed the fresh air and bright sun. He was nice, Claire thought. Smart. Funny. And yeah, handsome. Wow, maybe there's something to this stupid website after all. But then she asked what he did for a living—I'm a fertility specialist, he had said. Oh great, Claire thought, this guy is like super-smart, has all of this stuff going for him, and I'm just this average girl sitting across from him. They had a nice conversation and decided to head out after about an hour and a half. Jim walked her to her car and they exchanged a somewhat awkward hug. She thought, I don't even want to touch this guy. And when she got in her car, she realized why she didn't want to touch him: she would never see him again. He was definitely out of her league. It was a melancholy drive home, and she made sure of it by throwing in a Death Cab for Cutie CD. She drove mindlessly, her thoughts on why she was doing this online dating at all, how hollow and weird it all felt, when all she really wanted was someone to be honest with, someone to laugh with, someone who was authentic, someone to play with her hair. Someone to think of when she put her head down on the pillow, someone that just the thought of would make her smile and feel warm inside.

Her mind drifted as easily and airily as those fuzzy things you see in the air on summer days that you're supposed to wish on. She sorted through some of the dates she had had recently. The guy that shook her hand like a woman, who had ordered hot chocolate and then had chocolate all over his lips. The guy who couldn't really make eye contact, but could definitely stare at her breasts. The PhD in neurobiology from Yale, whose profile blew her away, who showed up at Barnes and Noble in carpenter shorts, a white polo shirt the sleeves of which had been cut off, and reeking of cigarette smoke, even though his profile indicated that he was a non-smoker. He was repulsive and actually a little scary. Glenn, the first of these weirdo match dates, who texted her the day after they met: "good morning princess." That took care of that pretty quickly. She shook her head, feeling tired and drained. She pulled into the apartment building she called "home for now" and took a deep breath. Everything will be ok, she whispered to herself.

The following day she received an email from Jim. She was stunned. And then really elated. He wanted to get together again.

Claire, I don't know why this is so hard for you to believe, Alex said.

Because, Claire replied, he just feels a little out of my league.

Fuck that shit, Alex replied eloquently. You are an amazing person and he'd be lucky to have you.

Thank goodness for friends, Claire thought.

Claire and Jim met for their second date at, shockingly, Café Atlantique. Jim had offered to drive down since they had planned on getting together earlier and Jim had had to bail. Work. So Claire thought, you can't choose when you are at your most fertile point, right? Gotta do things when the time is right . . . they were supposed to meet earlier that day to take his dog for a walk. In anticipation of meeting Jim's dog, Claire had purchased some organic dog treats. Claire loved animals, dogs especially, though she hadn't owned one since Smoky died. It had been hard for her to get over him, he was in a way her last connection with Douglas. But her mind was on Jim right now and when they met he put his arm around her right away. She liked that. He became more affectionate over the course of the evening, and it was delightful. When she gave Jim the dog treats, she said "I thought I was going to meet Charlie today, so I got him these treats" to which he replied, "Claire, that was really sweet of you" and he leaned over and kissed her. It was a quick kiss, gentle and soft, and Claire felt warm. Yum, she thought.

Their third date was dinner—Thai. They met after work in South Norwalk and walked around before deciding on Thai rather than Mexican. Claire's only problem with the dinner that night was that they were sitting too far away from each other. She wanted to be touching him in some capacity, and that's when she knew she was in trouble. They had a lovely evening and Claire drove home in somewhat of a daze, dizzy by spending time with someone she found smart, witty, authentic and handsome, and yet weirdly disturbed by her intuition saying "don't get too excited." She wondered if she was just always going to be super-cautious.

Don't sweat it, Claire, he obviously likes you, advised Alex. If he didn't, he wouldn't have kissed you on your second date, he wouldn't have asked you out for a third time, and he wouldn't have put his arm around you as you walked to your cars.

Thanks, said Claire, but still, I feel inferior. Like I'm not good enough for this guy.

Bullshit, explained Alex, That's insane. You are amazing and he knows it and that's why he wants to see you again.

In fact, they had made plans for the following week, Thursday. Claire wasn't sure what they would be doing, but it seemed as though Thursdays were good for Jim. She didn't think of asking why Thursdays must not be a fertile day for the patients he saw. Whatever, Claire thought, she was having a good time and should just relax. But part of her, for some reason, just couldn't.

The following Thursday they made plans to meet at his house and make dinner together. Claire found that to be somewhat intimate, but that did nothing but make her happy. They met at his home and made pasta, salad, and steaks. She met the dog and he took a liking to her—thank goodness Claire was saying to herself. Nothing like having the dog not like you. At one point she was playing with Charlie and Jim walked by and gently tapped her butt. It was so gentle and familiar that Claire wanted to cry. How sweet, she thought, how lovely this is. They had a nice night, great conversation and even a bit of snuggling on the couch. She didn't leave until after midnight. Getting up for work on Friday was miserable, but once she awoke, she remembered the night before, and a smile grew across her face the size of a cantaloupe. Wow, she thought, I really like this guy.

Once she got through date four, she told some other friends about Jim. They were all pleased with this news. Her friend Jenny from work felt that Jim must really like her to spend all this time getting to know her. Danielle said that he definitely liked her and that Claire needed to lighten up. Everyone though, was a bit perplexed at the lack of physical interaction. Aside from a few smooches, Jim and Claire hadn't done much, physically. Danielle said, hey Claire, maybe he's like you—he can't get there physically until he's there mentally. She laughed. But it wasn't really a joke.

Claire had always tried to be clear that she couldn't have a physical relationship until she had absolutely and firmly established a mental connection. She wasn't the kind of girl that was able to have sex with anyone "for fun." For Claire, physical connections meant that they had already had intense and meaningful conversations about life and honesty, and values and morals. She knew how it felt to just have a physical connection—hollow and unfulfilling and very lonely. How can you have a physical connection with someone without a mental one? To her, it meant just sex, which held no appeal. Sometimes she wished she could feel differently—or not feel at all, and just enjoy the pure animal connection. But she couldn't, and she had finally accepted that. It was good to know where she stood on the subject, and her feeling was, if I ever need sexual stimulation, if I ever need to have an orgasm, I have a hand, and a vibrator, and I can take care of business by myself. Still, she knew it was better with two.

Jim and Claire's fifth date was, in Claire's opinion, the best date of her life [at the time]. Which said a lot. She drove to Jim's house in excitement and anticipation. She went there straight from work, it was a Friday. She was finally starting to feel like maybe there was something to this. They planned to cook out at the local beach in Westport, the last day of summer that you could grill on the beach. It was a beautiful evening in October, prior to setting the clocks back. They cooked burgers and played bocce ball. While Jim was getting the charcoals prepared, Claire was assigned wine-opening duty. She was trying very hard to open the wine with a cheap wine opener that wasn't being very cooperative. As she was twisting with considerable might, the thin metal wine opener twisted and broke inside the cork. As she stared at it, a pit in her stomach formed at the thought of having to tell Jim. When she walked over to him, she said apologetically "Um, I'm not so sure about the wine." Why, he asked, and she showed him her work. He laughed heartily, and for the next ten minutes they tugged together at the wine and cork, finally pushing the cork through and pouring the wine in their plastic cups. They laughed and joked and it was so easy that Claire felt warm inside. It was nice being with Jim, she thought. I could get used to this.

The night got better. They ate their burgers from inside his jeep, since the wind was starting to pick up. It was just starting to get cold in the evenings and they both weren't used to it yet. In January, they would long for this weather, but right now it felt bone-chilling. They shared the fourth burger by exchanging it bite-by-bite, another thing that Claire found to be incredibly intimate. Jim took out his camera and began taking pictures of the beautiful sunset, the sky bright pink and violet, the sun the color of a canary. For a brief moment, Claire imagined hanging them on the walls of their home one day.

They went to pick up Charlie at the dog-sitters, and Claire was elated that the dog ran right to her and allowed her to pet and kiss him. She knew he was a friendly dog and that he was probably like that with just about everyone, but she pushed that out of her mind and just enjoyed it.

He really likes you, Jim said. Claire wondered if this guy also read minds. Why not, she thought, he has everything else going for him. She looked up at Jim and smiled.

Charlie sat on Claire's lap on the way home. (When she got home that evening, she would see the price she paid for that—her green sweater was covered in Charlie's white and black hair.) It was dark now, and chilly, and Claire wondered what they might do next. She wanted to kiss him, but felt awkward. He was so much fun, and had given clear signals at certain times, but he had not yet kissed her deeply or attempted anything that could be seen as a bit naughty. She figured she had actually met a male version of her when it comes to intimacy. Though her friends had been baffled.

He hasn't tried anything Claire, like you haven't really sucked face yet? Danielle had asked incredulously.

Not really, replied Claire. Maybe he's seeing someone else, or a couple of women, and he doesn't want to get intimate with anyone before he knows who he wants to spend more time with.

Well clearly he wants to spend more time with you, Danielle stated firmly. Claire, he's a busy doctor with his own practice, he calls you at strange times because he is always busy, but he manages to squeeze time in to spend with you.

Claire had a feeling in her gut that she was still suppressing, the one she had that first day she met him, driving home. Something just doesn't fit, she thought, and yet, she couldn't place her finger on it . . . so instead, she figured she would let go for once and enjoy her feelings and enjoy their time together.

When they got back to his house, Jim went to the kitchen and began putting the items away that they used at the beach. She thought it was funny when he said "don't do the dishes—Anna likes to do them." She laughed. Yes, I'm sure your cleaning lady is simply delighted when she sees a pile of dishes waiting for her, she said. They looked at each other for a minute and then laughed. He shrugged his shoulders "well, she never complains about it." Which Claire also thought was funny. How would an argument like that go? "Excuse me, I'm trying to do my job here but I really wish you kept your house cleaner."

He distracted her by saying "are you up for a cosmo" to which she replied "sure." "And let's play Spit now!" he said, quite enthusiastically. Claire found him to be adorable, because he seemed so genuine, and that was one of her fondest qualities in a person.

Claire taught Jim how to play spit in his dining room. He made sweet cosmopolitans with raspberry vodka. Having had some wine in her, and now the cosmo, Claire was slightly uninhibited. She was shouting "spit" left and right and while she wanted Jim to learn and understand it, she was too excited to let him win any hands. But he learned and he gained on her, and they laughed until they were almost in tears and just this simple evening of burgers, bocce balls and playing cards made Claire feel like all was well with the world. Here, tonight, in this comfy home, with this genuine man and his lovely dog, I am very happy.

Chapter 15

So I think we can safely say that you're dating him now, Alex said. Is that ok? I know how cautious you have been about it.

Claire said that after only four dates, she wasn't really sure that they could legitimately say that she was dating Jim. But, Claire said, I don't want to get hung up on that. The fact is, I really do like him.

You're *allowing* yourself to like him, said Alex, which is major.

Thanks, said Claire. And guess what? She said. I haven't dreamt of Douglas once in like six weeks.

Right on, Alex said, which Claire smiled to in agreement.

And how are you doing, Claire asked Alex, referring to her recent break-up with Bill.

I'm ok, Alex said in a rather sensitive voice, one that is trying to so hard to be careful not to break. Remember, she said, I'm superwoman.

Claire winced. She knew everything that Alex had on her plate and she wished that she could make it all better for her. She was such a wonderful person and there was no reason for all this crap to be piled her alone.

Chapter 16

Claire didn't hear from Jim for four days, and she began to get uneasy. Despite her friends telling her that he was "a busy doctor" she knew that it took two minutes to send an email, a text, or leave a voicemail. That gnawing in her gut again made its presence known and she started to consider what could be going on in The World of Jim.

Maybe he's delivering babies. Maybe he had to go to a meeting out of town. Maybe his dad's health condition worsened and he went home to see him. Maybe he's seeing a bunch of other chicks. That's the one that she went with. He's probably seeing other women, Claire concluded.

She walked downstairs the next Wednesday morning for some oatmeal. There was a heaviness in her step and she stopped halfway down the four flights of stairs and said out loud to no one "I'm tired." She was tired of guessing, tired of being alone, tired of pasting on a smile. She knew this, like all the other times that she momentarily wallowed, would pass. Still, at this very moment, she decided to allow herself this sadness and not, unlike usual, try to spring out of it with words of hope and encouragement and explanations that someone always has it worse than you.

Claire stopped to talk with her colleague and friend John Dover, who worked in internal communications. What's wrong, Claire, he said, you don't seem like yourself today. She smiled and looked at John. She was so happy to have him as a friend. He was probably about ten years older than Claire, in his mid 40s, and he had a kindness in his face that was rare. Claire felt like she could tell John her whole life story, like if the two of them were locked away for a week, they could tell each other everything about their lives and they wouldn't once judge one another. She thought that that's what it means to be someone's true friend. She looked at John, realizing that she had been somewhere else, and he was just patiently sitting there, also knowing she was somewhere else but would be back soon. I'm fine, Claire responded. It's 7:30 on a Wednesday morning and I have some oatmeal. I'm happy.

She went back to her office and set aside her oatmeal, deciding instead to read her email. She started to reply to a message from her boss when her cell phone rang. She looked at the time on her computer. 7:37. Who on earth would be calling me at 7:37 in the morning, she thought. It must be Alex.

But actually, it was Jim. And he was so sweet. Are you driving to work, he asked. Claire said, no, I've been here since 7:15. Wow, Jim responded. They exchanged some small talk and then Jim said "Um, Claire, I need to say something to you." Claire swallowed hard, realizing that he was probably going to try to let her down easily. He continued, Sometimes I drop off the face of the earth, I know, and I'm sorry. It's just that my work is really busy. But I want you to know that everything is cool. *Really* cool. Ok? Ok, Claire replied quietly, feeling like you do when you narrowly miss a bad accident. Adrenaline rush followed by limp exhaustion. They made plans for that Friday night, he asked if it was ok if they ordered in and watched a movie, and maybe went for a dip in the hot tub.

The words "hot" and "tub" combined made Claire instantly uneasy. Of course, she said, knowing that she would have to eventually get over the fact the she didn't exactly love her body in a bathing suit. Even though she knew she looked ok, she was never really perfectly happy with her body. But who is, she asked herself. She looked around at her desk after they ended their conversation and there was a lightness to her. She knew it would be a productive day, but first she needed to go downstairs and tell Danielle about the call she had just received.

A dip in the hot tub! Danielle exclaimed. I know, Claire said, rolling her eyes. Please, Danielle said, you'll look great. Will you wear a bikini? Claire laughed. Yes, unless I want to wear a Speedo from my high school days . . . and they burst out laughing. Claire imagined how embarrassing that could be and soon she was happier than a clam and didn't have a care in the world about wearing a bikini. He likes me, she thought. Everything is cool. *Really* cool.

Chapter 17

Again, they met at Jim's, and by this time Claire was feeling comfortable in the kitchen, getting out pots and pans, knowing where the olive oil was, seeing the honey she had purchased for their salads in the cabinet, and knowing how hot his water got. Things were feeling familiar to her and she felt like maybe she was ready to tell him a bit more about her life and her past. He had never asked her why she got divorced, in fact, he had never acknowledged that he even knew she was divorced. Claire thought it was a little odd but she had shrugged it off, knowing that there was a time and a place for everything, feeling proud that she had taken her friends' advice and not gotten into anything too deep or heavy right away. She instantly thought of Joe, the guy she had dated briefly in the beginning of the year. How she had told him on their second date that her dad had been an alcoholic and a pothead, that she was divorced because her husband cheated on her, and that she had huge trust issues. Poor Joe, she thought, I had to have scared him away by all of that. They had met one day in a group of cyclists, and Claire made a mental note that she needed to get on her bike this weekend to enjoy the fall foliage and brace for the winter hiatus.

Jim and Claire made dinner together: Claire handled the salad and pasta while Jim made steaks on the grill. When she went outside to sit with him as the steaks continued to cook, she noticed what was right across from the grill: the hot tub. Her apprehensions associated with the pending swimsuit exhibition had melted away though. They smiled and laughed and talked about work, their families, greek mythology. She silently thanked match.com for bringing her to this incredible person. Who else would discuss Aeneas and Dido with her, aside from Ken Schwartz, her old high school Latin teacher?

Jim was talking about work over dinner. They had opted to sit outside because it was a relatively warm night for the first week of October, and they both wanted to enjoy every last bit of warm weather they could. He was telling Claire about the couples that would come to his practice wanting to have a baby to save their marriages. Claire shook her head and felt a lump in her throat, and wondered if it would be a good time to tell him about the whole issue she had with Rick. That two years into their marriage, Rick had decided that "it wasn't part of the deal" for he and Claire to have kids. And that for almost five years, he would go back and forth—changing his mind—yes we can have kids on a Friday, no we can't on a Sunday morning—over cereal. Claire realized in retrospect that he only went back and forth externally. Internally, he had known he would never have more kids—probably before they had gotten married. He just pretended to be conflicted to confuse Claire. And she wasn't bitter about it, looking back. She had her perspective as well as Patty Blake's and some of her very close friends. She was ready to open her mouth and tell Jim when he leaned over out of the blue and gave her a sweet, small kiss. They sat with their faces close together for a moment and smiled at each other. And then he leaned back and yelled "Charlie, come get some food!" And she realized that the opportunity to mention Rick had passed, that she didn't get to tell him that her ex-husband had basically controlled the baby decision for her, that he cheated on her during that time, and the biggest blow—that he married someone else less than a year later and had a baby with her. The timing wasn't right now, but Claire finally felt at ease; that there would eventually be a right time with Jim. She believed that now, as she knelt down and played with Charlie. Good dog, she whispered.

Chapter 18

Later, on the couch, she found herself in between Jim and Charlie. She lightly petted Charlie's smooth hair and slowly he fell asleep. Jim, on the other side, sat closely, and held his arm gently around her waist. It was comfortable, and Claire thought of bringing up heavy stuff, but decided against it, because it was warm and calm and quiet. They were watching a documentary about beavers and discussing the amazing nature of nature. Claire's hand was resting on Jim's leg, and she squeezed him and said, Look at Charlie, he must have been tired . . . he is out! To which Jim softly responded, I'm a little tired myself. Claire tensed and said, I'm sorry, do you want me to go? Jim said No, emphatically, Just give me a few minutes he said, and with that, he nuzzled into Claire's shoulder. Besides, he whispered, I still want to go in the hot tub with you. Moments later, he was softly snoring, more heavy breathing actually, with a little nasal tone. Claire found it endearing. She smiled. Looked at the TV, at her hand on Jim's leg, and at the dog, whose fur she was still raking her hand through. Ok, she thought, pinch me.

Jim dozed for about fifteen minutes, and upon awakening, decided that it was time for the hot tub. By then, Claire felt so comfortable that she had no qualms about sporting her bathing suit.

Jim looked at Claire and said somewhat coyly, You should know, bathing suits are optional in the hot tub. Claire giggled. Please, she thought, just getting my head into a place where I can be ok with wearing a bathing suit—you have no idea. I'll opt to wear mine, she said, with a laugh.

The evening ended on a high note, Claire thought. After the hot tub, they both showered (separately) and met up in the living room, where they watched an episode of Nip/Tuck. It was disturbing yet intriguing, and she was glad that he felt the same way that she did about the show. At one point, there was a woman cheating on her husband, and Claire, laying on the couch with her head on Jim's lap, said quietly, Do you think that anything about this show is realistic? To which he quickly replied, Yes. Infidelity rocked my world. This stuff happens. She wanted to turn over and hug him, and say, I know it happens, it happened to me too, I get it, I can relate. Instead, she squeezed his leg as if to say, I understand, but maybe it was received as, I'm sorry. She wasn't sure and didn't feel like she should overanalyze. She figured there would be more time to understand what he went through, and for her to share what she went through, and when he walked her to her car, they exchanged a kiss and a hug and stood for a minute looking at the open sky, full of stars. Infinite possibilities, thought Claire. You never know where you're going to end up.

She was halfway home when she realized she wasn't listening to any music. A rarity for Claire. She smiled and popped in the closest CD, Ryan Adams' "Heartbreaker."

Chapter 19

After providing painstaking detail to Alex about the sixth date with Jim, Alex said, Claire, can we now say for good that you are officially dating this guy? Please.

Claire smiled. I think so, she said.

She realized that she hadn't been excited about anyone in quite a long time. She had been married for seven years and they had dated for a year beforehand. She had been divorced for four years, and hadn't really met the right guy during that time. Not like she was looking. In fact, it was the furthest thing from her mind. Once, her friend Dan had said, Claire, everyone has sexual needs and urges, it's ok if you just want to sleep with someone. To which Claire had responded, I know we all have needs and urges—thank goodness we all have hands. Dan looked at her quizzically. I can take care of myself, is what I'm saying, Claire said. Dan looked shocked. And Claire had started to think: I wonder if it's relevant that I say I can take care of myself. She wondered if she was so afraid of commitment that she wouldn't get close to anyone to find out if abandonment followed her. Like some dark shadow lurking fifteen feet behind her, wanting her to get involved with someone, so that he could come in and pull the rug from under her feet. Of course he is gone, Abandonment would shout, What did you expect?

Um, hello, helloooooooooooooooooooooo Clairabelle? Alex was saying, waving her hands in the air. Wow, this guy really has you reeling, huh?

Claire laughed and explained, I *was* somewhere else, to which Alex replied, Yeah, I know where you were. In fact, Alex had no idea where Claire had been, but Claire was feeling too happy and light to start in on a conversation about abandonment. It would be the perfect opportunity for Alex to roll her big brown eyes and say, Girlfriend, I'm worried about you. And she would have every right.

This time, Claire was determined to have a different attitude. *I am worthy of being with Jim, he is lucky to have me, we get along great and there's no reason to feel otherwise.* The tiny little gnawing in her gut was trying so hard, but she suppressed it with all her might. *Not this time,* she said quietly.

Chapter 20

That evening, Claire dreamt that she was driving down a road in the middle of the night. It was a dark and winding road and Claire had to really focus on her driving. A car came around the bend and it startled her. She swerved as it approached, not realizing how far she had gone into the other lane. But it was too late. She hit the car—brushed it, really, and each car's driver side was dented in. Broken headlights lay in the road, and Claire got out of her car, dazed and shaking. The man in the car she hit also got out of his car. He was Hispanic, heavy set, and looked to be in his mid-forties. He had long black hair that almost reached his shoulders, and a thick mustache. Claire was afraid. She was alone, it was dark and deserted, and she felt like running. But when he approached her, he said in the sweetest voice, Are you ok? And she nodded, but she wasn't ok, she was scared and it was dark and she wanted to wake herself up. Wake up! She shouted silently, pointlessly. He came to her and said, I'm Raoul. Don't worry. I'll take care of you. And her nervous energy seemed to flow from the top of her head and the bottom of her feet to a central location in her tummy, where it condensed itself and seemed to fly out of her body. She felt at ease. Raoul seemed to be saying something to her, but Claire was looking at the sky. Thousands of shooting stars were darting across the sky in front of her. She thought for a moment: what is the appropriate etiquette of telling a stranger whose car you just hit to look up at the sky? And then she just heard herself say, shooting stars, Raoul. Isn't it beautiful? He looked at her and she held his gaze. His eyes were black as night and they were so kind: she just knew he was a good person. He looked at Claire and said, Those aren't shooting stars, what you're seeing is fireworks. And she looked again, and realized that he was right. And it made her sad. She looked at him imploringly and he said, Things aren't always as they seem. Sometimes we see things just because we want to.

She awoke with a feeling in her gut that she couldn't shake all day. Something wasn't right.

Chapter 21

Claire was busy at work that week. There had been a "crisis" of sorts, not that Claire ever really found their media issues to be crises. A crisis is relative. *We aren't performing brain surgery*, she would often think to herself. In general, she felt that there was a lot of duplication of efforts at work. She felt like she could do her job from home most days. She felt like maybe her colleagues took things too seriously. Nevertheless, she enjoyed her work and felt grateful that she never went to work feeling grumpy or miserable about it.

Five o'clock arrived and Claire couldn't believe it. When hours feel like minutes—that feeling is supposed to be reserved for things that you love—for Claire, that would mean cycling, snowboarding, writing and developing photographs in the darkroom. But the day really had slipped by, it had been a productive day, and yet it was another day that Jim had yet to call. So she called him. She figured, why not, I can call him at this point. That thing in her stomach continued to eat away at her and she was annoyed. I'll show you, she thought. I'll call him and he'll be happy and we'll make plans to get together again. She got his voicemail.

The following day she was concerned. You are way too high-maintenance, Claire, said Danielle. Claire was hurt. She certainly wasn't high maintenance. She just liked to know where she stood with people. Is that too much to expect, Claire asked. Danielle admitted that Jim was somewhat inconsistent in his communications. But, Danielle reminded her, He's a doctor and he's busy. Besides, just remember: *everything's cool—really cool*. Whatever, Claire said, I have to go to a meeting in the boardroom and I can't be worried about this right now.

And in the boardroom, she was professional and focused, and she spent three hours discussing clinical data and appropriate messages for specific audiences—media, consumers, physicians, employees. They developed a communications plan and she got approvals from her medical colleagues, her German colleagues, and even the most senior of management, the boardroom for whom is just another conference room. She was pleased, and although the turnaround time for her to make revisions and distribute the materials to the larger group was tight, she felt like it was doable. She had time to get some water and make a stop at the bathroom, she assured herself, and then she could probably whip through her work. And as she was walking and playing the course of events for the rest of her afternoon in her head, she stopped abruptly. She knew at that moment that Jim had emailed her—and it wasn't what she wanted to hear.

Sure enough, she logged onto her personal email account when she got back to her office. Claire, she warned herself, you really need to get this done, everyone is waiting for it. But inside her, she knew she needed to check, that she wouldn't be able to pay attention to her work until she at least checked. And there it was. An email from Jim with the subject: *got your message.* Ok Claire thought, that could mean: Got your message, thanks, I've just been really busy, but I will call you tonight. Hope you're doing great. Or it could mean something else. For a moment Claire wondered if she could will it to be one way or another. She thought often about the universe and our own power to make things happen and our influence on people's behaviors and yet she knew she didn't have time for this so she said, Open the flippin email, Claire, and get it over with. It read:

> *Hey there Claire, Been giving everything some thought. I like to be truthful and honest. I just don't think this is clicking for me. I think you are a great person and have definitely enjoyed spending time with you. Good luck in all your endeavors. Jim*

Claire sat there suspended in time for a moment. She felt numb and she felt sad. She felt like all the blood had been drawn out of her body, and she read and re-read this brief note over and over again. The only thing she noticed was that the gnawing inside of her, that uneasiness, was gone. It's as if the email was the only proof it needed, and now it was released to go torment someone else. Or warn someone else. She tried to think of what she would say in return. Out loud she said, You mean I didn't get the job? *Endeavors?* Good luck in all your *endeavors?* How cold and impersonal. I don't get it, she thought, but she didn't have time to think about it, she had work to do and she was grateful for that.

That night, she went home and worked out and thought about the conversations that she and Jim had had during that last date. She recalled a lot of laughing, a nice dinner, no heavy conversation . . . well, when she asked him what superhero he would be if he could be any of them, he replied, Superman and when Claire asked why he had said, Duh, because Superman could do *anything*: he could fly, he had x-ray vision, he was really strong, for God's sake, he's the Man of Steel! They laughed. And don't forget he could turn back time, Claire had added. Good one, Jim responded. When he asked who Claire would want to be, she said, Wonder Woman, to which Jim replied, Because of the outfit? Claire had chuckled and said, Well, of course. But really, I always thought it would be neat to have the golden lasso of truth, she said quietly.

Ahh, so you have trust issues, he said, from the other side of the kitchen counter. He was preparing a pomegranate for them to enjoy. They had just discussed the myth of Demeter and Persephone and they simultaneously remembered the pomegranate that Claire had brought over.

Not really, Claire said quickly. Well, I mean, I always thought it would be a neat thing to have, even when I was a little girl. That you could just wrap a rope around someone and get the truth. She felt instantly bad: of course she had trust issues, but did she need to get into that now? They were having so much fun. It would have been such a buzz kill.

She started typing an email before her brain could even register that she was typing. Be careful, it warned, remember Patty Blake's concept of the unsent letter, remember not to write when you are very emotional, or if you do, save it as a draft. Sleep on it and if you still want to, you can send it in the morning.

Claire wrote:

Hi Jim,

Thank you for your honesty. I feel compelled to tell you that when I talked about wanting Wonder Woman's golden lasso of truth the other night, I really should have been more straightforward about the fact that I do have trust issues. So more than anything, I value honesty and truthfulness. I know bringing that up may seem strange, but I really like to be clear with people and really want that in return. So it lingered with me and I just wanted to say it.

I trust my gut a lot and was confused by some inconsistency in our communications—so I wasn't terribly surprised by your email. My gut told me you weren't there, but at the same time, I felt like when we got together, we did connect. It takes me a little while to get to know someone and feel comfortable enough to open up about certain things. It was refreshing to be with someone who was authentic and not looking to be anything other than that. Spending time with you was fun and easy, and surprisingly very comfortable given the amount of time we actually spent together.

So lest I drag this out (you may have already realized this tendency of mine to sometimes overcommunicate): I'm disappointed, but the chemistry and emotion of all this stuff is hard to explain and hard to understand sometimes. It was lovely to meet you and I wish you all the best too.

Claire

And before she could allow herself to think, to analyze, to wordsmith, she just hit send. It is what it is, Claire told herself. Now move on.

Chapter 22

Her first order of business was to remove her profile from match.com. She would wait a week, just because she didn't want it to be a dramatic response to feeling crushed. But when she did finally take the time to analyze, she realized that she was this upset because she had finally felt like there was someone with whom she would *want* to connect, someone out there that was fun and funny, witty and charming in a genuine way, someone she looked forward to seeing, someone smart and gentle and down-to-earth.

Oh well, Claire had said, when she told Alex that night she had received the email.

His loss, was Alex's response, and pretty much the response from her other friends. Everyone agreed that it was kind of lame that he didn't call her. After six dates and all that time they spent together, it seemed only appropriate. Claire was annoyed. She thought of the Seinfeld episode where Elaine wanted to break up with some guy on the phone, and Jerry said, if you haven't had sex yet, you can. And she winced. She hadn't come close to getting physical with Jim and she wondered if that's why he became disinterested. She hadn't offered up her philosophy on being intimate with anyone, but whatever, she thought, why analyze? It's not going to make him change his mind. And, she reminded herself, you want to be with someone who *wants* to be with you. If he doesn't, that's ok. Not everyone is going to like you that way. Unlike usual, Claire did not want to discuss this in depth with her friends. I'm tired, she heard herself saying inside, I'm just tired of caring, of wanting to care, I am ok on my own, I should just let this feeling envelop me, let it serve as a shield, recoil Claire, recoil, this is where you are most comfortable anyway. And for a minute she thought, Oh no, I won't see Charlie again.

Chapter 23

Before she went to bed that night, she wrote in the journal beside her bed, which was mostly intended to jot down dreams in the morning, before they evaporated. She liked to work through their meanings and try to make sense of them. Tonight though, this was what she felt compelled to write:

Nothing is right
No, not wrong,
Just not right
Off
I'm off balance
Off kilter
Something's not right
I'm half a person
I'm half on
I'm half of who I used to be
I turned something off inside
It's easier that way
I want to scream
I want to cry
I want to start over
What is right?
What is wrong?
What about fate?
What about destiny?
What about living?

I have to be true to the me inside
She deserves that much
But I don't even know if I know her anymore
And I'm afraid

Ugh, she thought. I better be able to sleep tonight.

Chapter 24

Claire slept soundly, and awoke with surprising clarity and peace of mind. She drove to work calmly and knew what she would do. It was as if the universe had whispered in her ear all night: Claire, you need to leave, you need to go away for a while, you need to be by yourself. Go somewhere alone, compose yourself, find *you* again, find what's real to you.

She got to work at 7:30 and by 8:00 she had found a great bargain on Travelocity. She emailed her boss and asked for the week off, which was just two weeks away. He had emailed back within minutes: Sure. So she was all set. She booked her tickets without thought, I am doing this, she said, I am doing this and it will be good for me.

Chapter 25

Claire called Alex that afternoon and said, Hey, I'm going away in a couple of weeks. Alex said, where to? And Claire replied, Copenhagen. Copenhagen, Alex had responded in a quizzical way. What the hell for, some Danish medical meeting? Do you think they really serve Danishes there? That would be funny.

Claire said, No, no medical meeting, I'm just going to get away for a little bit, nothing too exciting, I've just always wanted to visit Copenhagen and it's a good deal, and I figured, if not now, when?

Alex said, Wait. Let me get this straight, sister. You are going across the world by yourself? Because you *found a good deal*?

Claire replied quietly, I just want to get away for a little while. I'm tired and confused and I just want to go somewhere.

Oooooooooooooook, Alex said, but again, do you have to go that far away?

I want to, Claire said.

Fair enough, was Alex's response.

Chapter 26

Claire found herself waiting to board her connecting flight feeling uneasy and lonely. Well crap, she thought, I should finish this letter to Douglas once and for all, Patty Blake can stop harassing me about it and I can put it in the rear view. She thought to herself, Claire, you're using that phrase too much. I know you like it, but really, enough.

As she put pen to paper, she found that she wasn't writing to Douglas, but rather, she sat doodling pictures of airplanes and thinking:

Sometimes you can feel so alone. In a sea of people, yet connected to no one. No one knows me here, she thought, no one knows me. Then again, she would come to wonder that at various times in her life. How do you really know someone? Can you ever really be so connected to someone that they know you—all of you—inside, out, and that you know them? That someone could look into your eyes and understand you. That someone would know every dimension of your being. Someone who knew every line, every curve, and every subtle color of your eyes. Was it possible? How many people are together but don't even really know the other person? If we're only here once—and no one wants to be alone—shouldn't we aspire to find someone that wants to know us at a profound and deeply connected level? So that when you go to bed at night, you do so knowing that you are not alone in this world. That you matter to someone, and that you share something so unique and private that it can never be duplicated. Imagine how amazing that must feel.

And so tonight she felt alone. She didn't feel the energy of the airport. There were times when airports were magical to her—families reconnecting, friends taking trips, businessman in crumpled suits rushing to tend to "urgent business matters" (what were they running from, she often wondered). Families, she liked watching families the best. Grown adults hugging their becoming-frail parents. Children dancing around their parents, excited by the adventure of a pending trip—there were times when she would sit in wonderment and watch people and generally feel the joy of being among this microcosm of sorts. Noticing the nuances of smiles, the variety of different clothes based on the climate one just came from, the way people looked at each other, hellos and goodbyes, the way a husband would lovingly and without thought place his hand on the small of his wife's back, the laughter that prompted her to laugh out loud herself, the juxtaposition of the slow-moving old man in his white tennis shoes and Member's Only jacket and his bubbly granddaughter, bouncing airily around him in her flowered dress, her long crazy hair flying in every direction. Young and old. Happy and sad. Kind and bitter. Authentic and superficial. We're all different, but we're all connected, she would think, and the only way to explain that is—divine.

But tonight did not feel divine, tonight was actually quite sad. She didn't feel like she belonged anywhere. She was alone, and the buzz of people around her felt less vibrant. Around her, she saw strangers, blank faces showing no interest in smiling or even pretending to smile. Cold and isolated. She sat alone at an unoccupied gate and checked email. Sent a few text messages. Connections, please. She looked at her book, as if to try to decide if reading would help. Looked around. Felt alone. Analyzed it for a while. The realness of it scared her and she wondered how long she could sit there before the world forgot about her. She got up and walked the length of the terminal, trying to quiet her mind. Shake it off. If I fill it with other things, my mind will be occupied and I will not have to think about this loneliness. (She thought that was one of life's biggest tragedies—trying so hard to preoccupy yourself with something, burying whatever you need to work through, sublimating to a point where you wake up one day and don't even know who you are anymore.) Walking seemed to do little to help so she went to her gate—crowded, loud and bustling, she sat down in one of the few available chairs, hoping the crowd would revive her somehow. But again, nothing. No connections. Nothing to move her. The darkness of nothingness covered her, cornered her, wouldn't let her go. She felt cold, a heaviness in her gut.

And then she looked up. There was an old man sitting several rows beyond her, with bright white hair, his face painted with years of wisdom and the palest blue eyes, that almost translucent blue that only comes with age. He wore a red and blue checked shirt, button-down, short sleeves. Tan pants, belted too high at the waist. The stereotypical white leather sneakers for men of his age. A classic "q-tip." He sat quietly with his wrinkled hands folded neatly in his lap. She studied him, entranced, and he caught her gaze. And then he smiled at her. A wide, genuine, kind smile. A smile that made her heart swell. Like the grinch's when it grew three sizes. Poing! How cool. Thank you, mister. Thank you.

Chapter 27

Claire stepped off the plane feeling tired and weird. What am I doing, she thought, with a heavy sigh.

The Copenhagen airport was beautiful, wood floors, minimalist furniture, It looks like someone likes Ikea here, she commented to herself, and then laughed at her foolishness. Duh Claire, she said, you're in freaking Scandanavia.

The cab ride to the hotel was lovely. It was a dark, crisp night, and Copenhagen was illuminated. Huge old buildings towered around her and the streets seemed from another lifetime. It was rich with history, and Claire imagined all of the things that had happened there, all of the past; it made her feel insignificant.

Claire's hotel had the best bed she had ever laid on, a big fluffy, white down comforter and even mood lighting by the bed, courtesy of a dimmer on two of the smallest lights she had ever seen. This is lost on me, she said aloud to the hotel room, I'm here alone. But thanks anyway, she laughed.

She took a long hot shower in the see-through shower and settled into the comfy twin-sized bed. She turned on the TV and listened to the Danish translation of NYPD Blue. It made her laugh. She also liked to watch the Spanish channel at home sometimes, like National Lampoon's European Vacation en espanol, or Elf. She got a kick out of that. But geez, she thought, this language is tough to understand. And with that, she was fast asleep.

A morning run out of the way, Claire proceeded to the breakfast buffet and had some oatmeal, orange juice, and black coffee. She was tempted to eat some nutella but passed. She sat and looked at maps and things to do that the concierge had provided her when she came back from her run. She had seen several beautiful buildings and was excited about the day ahead. She almost forgot that she was alone.

And so Claire spent her five days in Copenhagen visiting old buildings, museums, historic castles, Tivoli Gardens, the Little Mermaid. She saw a lot and was thrilled that no one seemed to mind that she didn't speak a stitch of Danish. She dined on lobster bisque and yummy salads on Nyhavn Street and drank more coffee than she should have. It was delicious. She didn't pass on the chocolate scones, reasoning that she ran every morning and was entitled to a treat. She walked around alone but was so caught up in the people and things around her that she didn't care. She took pictures and enjoyed the cool weather and walked for hours.

The Little Mermaid amused her. Here, this famous sculpture, just sitting in the water. And busloads of people come from afar to see it every day. Indeed, there had been two busses of seniors that came while she was there. She took a picture of an old man in his oversized baseball hat, who was having his picture taken, maybe by his wife, as he stood as close to the Little Mermaid as he could. He was beaming, and Claire thought, I hope I am happy about this kind of stuff when I am his age. He looked so content, and it made her feel warm inside.

Tivoli Square was strange, a big amusement park with random shops, and every store seemed to sell a lot of licorice. There were a lot of families there, and Claire found out that Saturday is *Family Day*, and that so many people would be there because all the stores in Copenhagen are closed on Saturdays. It forced people to spend time with their families, she reasoned, but as she observed people, she noticed that they seemed thrilled to be with their spouses and children. Little girls were dressed up as princesses because apparently, they got in for free if they dressed as princesses that day. They had theme/costume days at Tivoli. It was cute, and everyone there seemed to be having such a genuinely good time. She watched a play in Danish on a small stage, which was obviously about a princess, and all of the children were mesmerized. The princess invited children on stage and parents took photographs, while socializing with friends. Claire thought that she hadn't seen anything so lovely in a long time, and she thanked the universe for getting her to Copenhagen to see this and be part of it. Family time: what an underrated concept.

When it was time to leave, she packed her bags while listening to TV—it was Cheers in Danish and she was again amused. She looked around and thought about the few days she had been there. It was long enough, and yet it wasn't, she thought. Long enough to clear her head a bit and realize that life is . . . a series of hellos and goodbyes, she sang to herself. No, that life wasn't about things being perfect, and things hadn't felt perfect with Jim, she just wanted them to. Life is about now, enjoying the moment, enjoying your friends and family, and being true to yourself. No one can ever fault you for that, Claire, she told herself. She walked to the door and looked around, smiled, and dimmed the lights. I'm going home, Claire told her hotel room.

Chapter 28

Claire was happy to be home, good old Bradley Airport, she thought, there's something so comforting about that which is familiar. She got her bags, found her car, thought, Brrr, it's freezing here, what happened? and got to her car. Hi Car, she said, It's good to see you. She turned the ignition and Neil Young was singing Old Man to her. Yay, Old Man, she thought, but she also recalled the way she was feeling on her drive to the airport, and so she took out the CD and deciding that rather than listen to music, she would call her friends, reconnect, tell them about her trip. Surprisingly, she cared less about sharing the details of Copenhagen and more about what had been going on back home.

Danielle had been promoted to Executive Director of Marketing for the brand she worked on.

Lyndsay had made significant progress with her wedding plans: videographer, photographer, and florist all confirmed.

Susan had started seeing the guy from the gym that she liked. It was finally official, they had had two dates while Claire was in Copenhagen.

And Alex had had her biggest month at work, and found an amazing new apartment that was right on the water. And she'd had an incredible facial and massage, which was not to be overshadowed by the amazing apartment.

Claire was happy for her friends. She felt tired as she traveled the Merritt Parkway in the dark. North Haven, Hamden, New Haven, West Haven, Orange, one more exit and I'll be home, in Milford. It'll be nice to be home. It *is* nice to be home.

When she finally checked her email, she had a sea of messages. None from Jim, but she wasn't surprised, and she was not dismayed. She just was. I am really ok, she thought.

Chapter 29

Claire invited the girls to meet and see her pictures, and it felt good to be hanging out with everyone. She felt like the trip had been good for her mentally. She was feeling as though she was really in a good place, more so than in a long time. Her friends were looking at her pictures and looking around at each other. Claire, Alex said, Copenhagen looks beautiful, but did you like, take a picture of every freakin building and every statue? The girls laughed heartily. Ha ha, Claire said, Maybe I did! I wanted to torture you by having to look at them, that's why I took lame-ass pictures.

They aren't lame-ass at all, Danielle said, They just look like they should be in an exhibit.

Well, remember everyone, I took a solo trip to clear my head. I wasn't exactly sightseeing with a tour.

Alex looked around. Claire's like the only girl I know who clears her head with a vacation somewhere cold and far away. What happened to the beach and suntan lotion and a trashy novel?

Claire was the first to laugh. She had thought of that after she made her reservations to Copenhagen. Why not just the beach, she thought? But she had needed to be distracted. She needed to not understand the language, to have to navigate a strange land. And besides, who can rediscover themselves in Miami?

Claire got up to get more wine and a cheese plate, and Alex wrapped her arm in Claire's arm, and they walked in that fashion up to the counter. In doing so, they bumped into a smallish, dark-haired man. His eyes looked vacant, but when Claire looked again, she saw that they looked sad, despondent, lonely. They made eye contact and Claire held his gaze. I'm sorry, we just walked right into you, she said.

It's ok, was his response. He returned to his seat at the coffee shop and ate his pannini alone, in silence. Claire felt sad for him, she hated to see people eat alone. She would wonder about his life, why he was alone, if he had ever been in love, what happened and why . . . she wondered why, at the end of the night, she still couldn't shake her thoughts of this short, slight man with the long face, greasy skin, greasy hair, and nails that had been chewed down so far it looked painful.

Chapter 30

In fact, that greasy man was Albert Palletti, a simple man, leading a simple life as a postal worker. He had delivered mail for close to forty years, his very first job out of high school. He had dreamed of becoming a writer, but needed an income to save for college. He wrote poetry and short stories in high school and his English teachers would all tell him how much promise and potential he had; they encouraged him to pursue his dreams and never to be discouraged—writing was a difficult process and one that took time and patience. He was young and excited about his future.

Albert's dad, Albert Senior, had worked at a local pen manufacturer, also right out of high school, but never saved money for his kids' college education—it was all he could do to simply pay the bills and put food on the table. Albert's mother was a homemaker, and raising him and his two brothers and two sisters was certainly a full time job.

Albert sometimes felt like Jimmy Stewart's character in It's A Wonderful Life. George Bailey's timing had always been off—he had wanted to do so many things as a young man, but he met obstacles every time he tried to get out of BedfordFalls. And so Albert felt that he could relate: he never got out of Milford, except for his brief stint in Branford almost twenty years ago, when he wanted a change of scenery and thought perhaps it would lead to a new position internally, reporting to the Postmaster General of the town. But the job never panned out, and so he returned to Milford. He married, sure, of course, everyone marries, right? A nice girl named Rita, she was kind and mild and made delicious lasagna. They loved each other, as much as they possibly could, though they never really spoke openly about their feelings, thoughts, desires, they never had children, and they spent many years eating dinner together at their formica kitchen table in silence. That's why Albert didn't mind eating alone at Café Atlantique. He was accustomed to it. Indeed, when Rita left him 23 years ago, he didn't miss her presence at the kitchen table. Just the food.

Rita had indicated her reason for leaving was because she felt "unfulfilled." Albert found out later that she had been having an affair with her boss. She was a legal secretary in New Haven, and so from that point on, Albert hated lawyers. Mail from legal institutions—they never quite made their way to the right places at the right time. Sometimes they would get lost or sometimes they would get stolen or oops, sometimes they ended up in the sewer. I wonder how that happened! Albert would exclaim, as he "accidentally" dropped pieces of mail through the sewer gates. He knew that what he was doing illegal, but he would say to himself, So sue me you shitheads. Federal offense my ass. Make my life worse, just go ahead and try. His laugh was both sad and bitter.

He broke from that thought when the two giggling girls strolling arm-in-arm walked into him. I wonder if they're lesbians, he thought, and he allowed himself to ponder that for a while, eating his ham and swiss pannini.

Chapter 31

Douglas made an appearance in Claire's dreams that night. It had been a while. This time he was cutting wood wearing a plaid shirt, she thought the name of it in the J Crew catalog was *black plaid*. Navy and green and, she guessed, black. He looked like he did in that picture she had of him and OB skiing. They were such good friends. He had sent her that picture in one of his letters when they lived apart, and when she woke up, she thought about the value of writing letters versus emails. There's something to be said for having something tangible, something to hold and to keep, knowing that the other person held it in his or her hands and rubbed their hands against it and folded it, placed it in an envelope and put it in a mailbox. But before she could think about that, she continued to dream. She approached Douglas as he was cutting wood. He was whistling, and Claire was smiling, because she loved it when he whistled—it meant he was content. He looked up as he was swinging his axe and saw Claire. He ran to her and hugged her, a deep, close, nothing-can-come-between-us hug. He pulled away only slightly and said happily, Did you get my letter?

Claire awoke hugging her blanket. It was all jumbled up in front of her and for a brief moment she actually thought she was hugging Douglas. When she realized she wasn't, she felt that deflated feeling when you've woken from a good, happy dream, only to come to find it was just a dream. She stumbled into the bathroom and brushed her teeth, and as she slowly replayed the dream back, she thought, I wonder what significance the letter has. *My letter? My **unsent** letter?*

Chapter 32

Claire and Lyndsay decided to meet at the coffee shop since it had been a while since they had gotten together, aside from hanging out together at the gym in spin class. And that didn't really count. Lyndsay took the train to work, and since the coffee shop was right near the train station, it seemed the most convenient location. Claire sometimes felt like she lived there, her home away from home, but then again, it was a great environment, the people were nice, and there was plenty of good food, good wine, and good coffee. What else mattered?

Lyndsay arrived as Claire was ordering their wine—I took the liberty of getting us the Rielsing, Claire said. I hope that's ok. Yay, say Lyndsay, and Claire looked at her and thought, This girl just doesn't have a mean bone in her body. She is sweet and genuine and I am so happy to know her and call her my friend.

They walked to a table chattering like schoolgirls and both stopped talking when they saw the guy two tables down. He was on his computer and appeared to be in deep thought. Wow, Claire said, he is handsome. Lyndsay agreed. You should go talk to him, she said, and Claire frowned. Good grief, like I should just walk up to him and say, Hi Handsome, whatcha working on there? Lyndsay laughed. These days it just felt entirely outrageous to talk to a stranger. Although Claire thought, how ironic that it's easier and more acceptable to talk with someone when you're in a bar, as opposed to a coffee shop? I mean, it's so less obnoxious to talk with someone in this kind of environment. It's amazing how alcohol can dull your inhibitions. And your judgment, she quickly added. Lyndsay was talking about his shoes. Yes, he has nice shoes, Claire agreed. And he has nice hair she said, and it was true, it was dark brown, perhaps one could say it was the color of dark chocolate, not to be mistaken for Claire's milk chocolate brown hair. He looked up and you could see his eyes were hazel, even though he wore black plastic rimmed glasses, and he reminded her of Clark Kent, when he was played by Dean Cain in The Adventures of Lois and Clark. He was boyishly handsome, and Claire was attracted to the brainy types more than anyone else. Alright Lyndsay, she heard herself saying, I have to stop looking at this guy. Tell me more about your wedding plans! Handsome Man had noticed Claire and Lyndsay and smiled to himself. It was nice to think that a couple of cute girls were checking him out, especially since he had just been dumped by his college sweetheart for a doctor. Honestly Adam, she had said, did you ever think I could live on your salary as a professor, the way I really want to live? When he came back to reality, the two of them were in deep conversation over their wine, and it seemed to him that everything and everyone around them had become a blur.

When Claire was leaving, she noticed that small man again, he was eating alone and staring into space. Hello, she said, and she obviously startled him. Oh hello, he replied, and went back to eating his sandwich. Claire felt oddly attached to him, as if they were somehow related, and she wondered if they were. She shrugged it off quickly as her being way too into the interconnectedness of all human life, of all life in general, and she kissed and hugged Lyndsay goodbye, stole a quick parting glance at the boyishly-handsome-brainy-looking guy, and walked home.

Chapter 33

On a cold, rainy Saturday morning, Claire made some coffee and sat down at her computer. She fired it up and pulled up the unfinished, unsent letter that she had begun writing to Douglas months back. She had been through some crazy dates, all that nonsense with Jim, a few "issues" at work, several sessions with Patty Blake, and yet the letter still sat there. She knew she was going to see Patty Blake this week and really wanted to make some progress. No, more than that: she wanted to finish it. So she sat in her pink-and-blue flowered pajama bottoms and pink tank top, grey oversized sweatshirt and warm, fuzzy socks, and with a hot mug of coffee at her side, she typed the end of her letter:

> Douglas,
>
> I stopped writing this for a while. I've been busy. I've had some ridiculous dates. I did meet one guy that I actually really liked. We had six dates. I thought everything was going well. He had a great dog. But for some reason, he told me it "wasn't clicking" for him. Ouch. Why is it that rejection never gets easier? I mean, in any capacity? Dodge ball team selection in gym class, the prom, work assignments, friends, potential lovers. Why is it that we experience rejection in some capacity throughout our lives, and we reject people in some capacity as well at various times, and yet, when it happens, we feel crushed? I guess that's just part of being human, right?
>
> You rejected me by leaving and never saying goodbye. And all these years have passed, and you never once looked me up to say hello. I mean, of course you have gone on with your life, but how easy would it have been to just google me and pick up the phone? I'm not hard to find. There aren't many Claire Cassidys

in Connecticut, and you could have figured I might have stayed here.

Are you thinking, It would have been easy to find me too? I imagine it wouldn't be too hard to find some Douglas Bachs in the world. We didn't have email and the internet back when we were dating, can you imagine growing up with it? But I digress. The fact is, I have never looked you up. I have been tempted, just so you know. But you left, you wanted to leave without saying goodbye, so I never really thought it would do any good to find you. What for, to ask you why? Who needs an answer to that? I mean, I would love one(I think), but just the fact that you left is probably enough. Yes, I am writing to ask why you left, but remember, I'm never going to send this letter. It will probably end up at the dump, or shredded in a bin at work, or maybe I'll burn it, or hey, maybe I'll put it in a bottle and throw it in the ocean! That would be rich. My very own message in a bottle. Maybe a wonderful man will find it as he is walking along the beach, and it will break his heart, and he will look me up and find me (because it's easy) and he will come to me and profess his love for me, and I will fall into his arms and . . . yeah I know, I can't even finish that thought. You know me, I am a realist. I have a hard time with that kind of crap. The fact is, I'm not asking you why you left, because I'm not waiting for your response. I'm writing this letter because my therapist thinks it will be therapeutic (that was sort of meant to be funny) for me. I dream about you still, Douglas. There are times when I miss you. There are times I hear your voice. In my dreams, you are crystal clear, I can remember every subtle nuance about you. Your smile, your gray eyes, your scent. Sometimes I go to bed at night praying for you to be in my dreams. Other times I curse you for showing up. Please, please let me go. I will never understand why you left, and I have to be ok with that.

I hope you are well and I hope that you are surrounded by friends and family and a lot of love. I hope that writing this letter will be helpful, and that you will fade from my mind. I hope that you still think of me sometimes. I hope you know how much I loved you.

Love,
Claire

P.S. Smoky died when he was 14. He had a great life. I used to take him hiking at Sleeping Giant and he loved sitting in the garden. He had an inoperable tumor in his kidney that spread quickly. I held him when he was put to sleep. I cried, but I knew it was best for him—he was really starting to suffer. I whispered to him that he would be ok, that I loved him, and though you had been gone for years, I told him that you loved him too. I thought you would want to know that.

Chapter 34

Albert was starting to get pissed that this girl with the long brown wavy hair and bright blue eyes was always staring at him whenever they passed by each other. What does that lesbo want with me, he thought. Although maybe she wasn't a lesbian, since he had seen her with men at times. She always smiled at him, and it made him feel uncomfortable. She had to be more than 30 years younger than him. Look at her, standing there, contemplating what kind of tea she wants. Make up your mind, bitch, and stop looking over at me. Claire did make up her mind, almost as Albert was thinking this, and she said, I'll have the Cardamom Cinnamon, that's delicious.

For a moment Albert stopped chewing and thought, I wonder if I did that. Imagine, I have that power to control people and I'm just now finding out. And before he could resume chewing, Claire flashed a kind warm smile at him, and he was instantly annoyed again. Annoyed because, Who does she think she is, smiling at me? And annoyed because in truth, it made him ache with loneliness.

Go away, he thought, I'm no good, I'm unlovable, my wife left me for a lawyer, when I don't eat dinner here, I eat frozen dinners in my sweatpants and undershirt. I'm a tired man with nothing to give. I never had much to give anyway, come to think of it. I guess I could give you some mail. That's about it. He smiled at himself and stared out the window, watching cold commuters walk briskly in the dark from the train station to their cars. I could give you some mail.

Claire took her tea to go—she was meeting her new friend Jack, the 24 year old accountant that she had become friends with after meeting him on Match. They had determined up front that their age difference was too significant to pursue a romantic relationship; and yet, they enjoyed hanging out together, and so they became friends. Claire was meeting

Jack in New Haven to go see Cinema Paradiso at York Square. It had been one of her favorite movies over fifteen years ago, and since Jack was only—well, since Jack was a kid then and hadn't seen it, and York was playing it again (not quite yet labeling it as a "classic" thank goodness), she said she would take him to see it. She had warned him that the movie was subtitled, and waited expectantly for the rumble and moan, Ugh, subtitles? But Jack simply said, Oh cool, I love the Italian language, that'll be fun. And so she felt further validated that it was good to be friends with this guy. Yay, she thought, a guy that likes subtitled movies. She corrected herself: a *friend* that likes subtitled movies.

After the movie she and Jack went to Koffee 2 and had caramel lattes. They talked about life and clothes, politics and the butterfly effect, movies and interior decorating. If Alex was here, she would call Jack a "cool cat." Alex could say things like that and get away with it. Claire loved that about her. In the meantime, she just looked at Jack and smiled at his effervescence, his truthfulness, his youth and his intensity. She thought to herself for a moment, If only you were ten years older. She sighed audibly, her hands cupping her face as her arms supported them on the table. Jack stopped mid-sentence and said, What was that all about?

What was what all about, Claire asked.

The sigh, he said, raising his eyebrows as if to say he was completely stating the obvious.

Oh, Claire removed her hands from her face. She had clearly appeared enthralled and needed to shake it a little.

Jack smiled and took Claire's hands into his. He kissed both hands and looked at her warmly. We'll be friends forever, he said, in a way that made her feel like he really believed it.

Chapter 35

Claire drove home from her afternoon with Jack feeling good about herself. Ever since her return from Copenhagen, she was starting to feel less . . . less . . . what was the word she was thinking? Less broken, she said aloud. I feel less broken. I should call and make an appointment with Patty Blake she said, also aloud, as though she was talking directly to the person in the passenger seat who did not exist. If someone saw here driving and talking like this, they may think she was a loon.

She decided to call Isabelle instead of talking to herself. She wanted to know how she was doing, she thought Isabelle had been training for a marathon in Chicago or something, but that couldn't be right, not as winter was approaching, that would just be cruel. And yet, Isabelle was cruel to her body. She worked out in the gym for hours after work, lifting weights and doing crunches and all sorts of abs exercises until she was completely ripped. And in the morning, she would get up early, when the wind was howling and the windows on cars were still covered in frost and pretty much everyone was still in REM sleep, and she would run for mile after mile. No music, just the quiet sound of her feet hitting the ground, left, right, left, right. Claire would worry that something was wrong, but Isabelle was strong and sensible and was capable of surprises. Just when her friends were convinced she had some sort of eating disorder, she would surprise them by eating a huge bowl of linguine.

But Claire couldn't really understand why she wouldn't date. It had been a couple of years since she and Mark had broken up. He was weird and verbally abusive and Claire wondered if he had been more than just verbally abusive. Claire corrected her thought: not *just* verbally abusive. It just seemed that Isabelle was so disinterested in meeting anyone at all. Though, on some level, Claire could relate. It had taken her a while to move past all the crap associated with Douglas. And Rick, of course.

Sometimes, she realized, it was better to be alone. And Isabelle would only reinforce her position on not wanting any boys in her life when they exchanged horror dating stories.

Claire got Isabelle's voicemail. She had put the phone on vibrate to concentrate on what she was doing: writing a letter to Chris.

Isabelle cursed Claire for making her think about the Unsent Letter. How lame is this, she thought. And yet, as soon as Claire had mentioned it at the coffee shop that night, Isabelle's heart sank. She knew it was time to break ties with Chris. She had been in a relationship with him for years without telling anyone, except her therapist. It was no wonder she had developed an eating disorder, she thought (which was cleverly kept from everyone, she thought proudly). She trained for marathons year-round, and would travel to different states throughout the year to take part in them. She would run until her toenails fell off, run in the dead of winter until her face was severely chapped, run until she sometimes didn't know where she was, run in the morning, run at night, just keep moving. She was unable to sit still, and her friends never understood the true driving force: not that she was an overzealous athlete, but that she was running, literally, from her life.

Well, Isabelle thought, I guess it's about time to bite the bullet and write this letter. It's time I moved on with my life. I'm 29, and I'll never get married or even give myself the opportunity to be in a normal relationship if I stay with Chris.

Dear Chris,

I'm going to be brief because I hate writing. But you know this is long overdue. Our relationship has been a series of compromises. Despite that, we saw all that was wonderful in each other, and even that which wasn't so wonderful, and we decided that we would accept the shortcomings to be able to experience a loving relationship.

My therapist told me that I was comfortable being in limbo and that I was comfortable with the fact that I knew someday things would end, that way I wouldn't be surprised. I knew there were people in your life that were more important than me, so I wouldn't be devastated when we had to disconnect. She was wrong, I do feel devastated.

Slowly I have been feelings the effects of our ambivalence as we try to figure out where to go from here. I feel like you are moving farther away from me a little each day, and sometimes I feel like I am sort of a security blanket for you. I guess maybe we are that for each other. When you've been so close to someone for so long, how do you voluntarily move away from that person? I know that the future is going to feel empty for a while, for both of us. I hope that we are both able to get through this knowing that it's for a bigger purpose. That thought will have to sustain me during some dark and lonely times ahead. And I hope you know that you will always have a very special place in my heart and I will never forget everything that you have been to me.

Now it's time. Time for me to put myself first. Time to heal. Time to get help, to start eating, and to stop running (in the proverbial sense, anyway).

Love,
Isabelle

Chapter 36

It was mid-November when Claire went for a long bike ride through the backs roads of Weston with Danielle. She road home, feeling like her legs were going to pop off, after she and Danielle had parted ways near Danielle's house. Weston, Westport, Fairfield, Trumbull, Stratford, and phew finally Milford, Claire said aloud, as she approached home. She got off her bike as she hit the CVS on Post Road. I am so thirsty, she thought, I need a water. She looked gross. Sweaty, matted hair, and just grimy from a day on the road. Feeling good, but sweaty. She didn't really care about how she looked, until she saw Handsome Guy from the coffee shop, the one that she and Lyndsay had seen a couple of weeks back. They made eye contact and she smiled a small smile, one that looks like it's out of politeness more than anything (it was really out of embarrassment). He looked at her for a moment before recognizing that it was the girl from the coffee shop that had been looking at him the other day. One of the girls that had been looking at him. The girl with the kind eyes. He thought she looked sweet. He smiled back. He wanted to say hi, but decided not to. Certainly she has a boyfriend or a husband, he thought, and he walked past her towards the card section.

Chapter 37

On a cold, gray morning in November, the week before Thanksgiving, Claire took a day off from work. She had to take days off or else she would lose them. So she planned a packed day: spin class in the morning, breakfast with Lyndsay, an appointment with the nutritionist, and an appointment with Patty Blake. She was feeling good overall and was happy to see Patty when she arrived at her office a little before 3pm.

Hi Dr. Blake, she said cheerily.

Hello, Claire, you seem quite happy.

I *feel* quite happy, Claire replied.

And so began their session, which Claire always found to be a little awkward. Small talk about the weather or the holidays or whatever, it just seemed somewhat contrived. In any event, Claire felt like it was a productive hour with Patty Blake. She told her about how things ended with Jim, her spontaneous trip to Copenhagen, and her new friend Jack. She was also delighted (and clearly a bit proud) to report that she had finished her Unsent Letter to Douglas.

Dr. Blake seemed perplexed about Jim's decision to end the relationship with Claire, upon which Claire interjected, Not a *relationship*, Dr. Blake, we had only had six dates. Patty Blake corrected her: regardless of the amount of time, he did end whatever you had, which was, by definition, a relationship. But, she said, Regardless, you seem to be moving in the right direction and have a healthy mindset about what happened between the two of you. I just feel compelled to say Claire, you know that it's not because you're inferior, right? I mean, I know he is a doctor and wealthy, and all of that, but you know you are worthy of someone's love and kindness, and it doesn't matter what they do for a living, how handsome they are, or how much money they make. You know that, right?

Claire smiled. I think so, she answered honestly.

That's fair enough for now, Dr. Blake said.

In terms of her new friendship with the 24 year old, Patty Blake said that it was nice, and she also said that Claire smiled a whole heck of a lot when she spoke about him. She tilted her head and smiled at Claire and said, You also know that you're allowed to have friendships with men that are younger than you, right? There is no reason to feel guilty about that.

Thanks, was Claire's response.

Dr. Blake sat for a moment as if to allow Claire any additional thoughts. OK, just a thank you, she thought. As for Copenhagen, she continued, It seems as though that was a very positive experience for you. You were obviously in a funk about Jim, and I know you were feeling depleted. I think it was a pretty gutsy thing for you to do, just pick up and take a trip like that. You put yourself first, and for that I am proud of you. You seem to have enjoyed it and you seem to have gotten some much needed down time. You seem calm and clear, maybe it gave you some perspective about where you have been and where you are headed. Do you think?

Kind of, Claire said as she shook her head.

Good, said Dr. Blake. So you finished the letter to Douglas. How do you feel about it?

Claire smiled. I feel really good about it, she said. Really good.

Why, asked Dr. Blake.

Well, Claire hesitated, unsure of her words. I just feel like it was nice to get all of that off my chest. I realized somewhere in the middle of writing it that I had written a similar letter to Rick, she admitted. I went searching for that letter to figure out if writing it had helped me in any way, she said. And when I re-read it, I . . .

She sat for a minute, biting her lower lip and staring at the marble paperweight on Patty Blake's desk.

You what, Claire? How did it make you feel?

Crummy, Claire responded.

How so? Dr. Blake countered.

Claire laughed a quiet, little, sad laugh and smiled. It's hard to describe. It . . . It made me want to hug the Claire that was then and tell her that eventually she would be in a much better, happier place.

Do you feel like you're in a much better, happier place, Dr. Blake asked.

I feel like I'm on my way, Claire offered. I'm working on it, she continued. I feel like I'm living authentically and I'm working through the Douglas Stuff. I feel like I'm past the Rick Stuff. I know you and I need to eventually get to my Dad Stuff, but overall, yeah, I feel like I'm moving in the right direction. And that makes me feel good.

Good, Claire, that's really good, said Dr. Blake.

They ended their session, and while Claire wrote out a check, they discussed plans for the upcoming holiday. Again, Claire thought, I like Patty Blake, but this just feels weird.

Chapter 38

Claire went home and made a jicama salad, one of her favorites. She spoke briefly with Alex about nothing in particular, took a shower, settled into her pj's, and got a call from Jack.

Perfect timing, she said.

Why is that, Jack asked.

I just took a shower and now I'm nice and clean, Claire said in her nighttime voice.

Yum, Jack said back. What's up with your voice?

Oh, Claire said, sometimes at night my voice gets a little tired and croaky.

Don't be sorry, Jack said, You sound hot.

Claire laughed. That's hilarious, she said.

Jack complained about his long day at work and recounted every diet pepsi and coffee he had had throughout the day.

You drink too much caffeine, Claire said in a way-too-maternal way.

And you looked really pretty the other night, Jack said, completely out of the blue.

Oh, my. Thanks, Jack. That's very sweet of you.

You're welcome.

They chatted more about the day and Claire mentioned that she'd been to see Patty Blake, her therapist.

Did you mention me to your therapist, Jack asked.

Claire made a face and she hesitated. Actually, I did, she said. Why?

No reason, Jack said. I'm gonna go and watch TV for a while, I need to decompress before I have to go back to work in the morning.

Alright, Claire said. Get some rest, and sweet dreams.

Sweet dreams to you too Claire, and I'm glad you told your therapist about me, even though I'm not sure why.

Bye Jack, Claire said, laughing as she hung up.

Bye hot stuff, Jack replied.

Chapter 39

On her way home from work, Claire went to the grocery store to get some stuff for Thanksgiving. She was making dessert. Chocolate bread pudding, one of her staple desserts. She turned down the baking goods aisle abruptly. When she went shopping, she usually timed herself. It was like a game for her: how quickly can I get in and out of the store? She stopped short when she saw The Handsome Guy from Atlantique. She imagined what she looked like after a day at work and an hour drive home. God, she thought, can I ever see this guy when I look halfway decent? Something about him made her a little warm inside. He turned and saw her, and smiled. She smiled back, and wondered what he was buying just days before Thanksgiving; his wife had probably sent him out to buy some last-minute necessities. Wait, no ring. His girlfriend then. Claire rationalized that someone that looked as cute as this guy surely had one or the other. She thought of saying something like, Have a nice holiday, but it felt contrived and she didn't want to seem weird. He was thinking the same thing, and so rather than make a connection at that point in time, in the Milford, Connecticut Super Stop&Shop just days before Thanksgiving 2006, they smiled politely and passed each other, each of them thinking "what if", each of them protecting themselves enough not to find out.

Timing is everything, thought Claire, as she went through the self-checkout.

Chapter 40

Claire and Jack were drinking beers in his kitchen. Claire was telling him about the tour she took of the Magic Hat factory in Burlington, Vermont. It was a freezing day, I was layered in turtlenecks and sweaters, coat, mittens, boots, scarf, she laughed.

But the beer warmed you up, I bet, Jack said.

Indeed it did, Claire giggled.

I feel toasty, Claire declared, as she hopped up onto the kitchen counter. She swung her feet happily and looked at Jack. What, he asked.

Nothing, Claire said. And smiled.

What? Jack asked again, coming closer to Claire's face. What are you laughing at, you silly girl?

Can you just put some good music on, please??? She said. Something other than this crappy rap stuff.

Oh, you don't like my music, he said mockingly. Nice, Claire. Yes, let me find my 80s music. I think I have a few *cassettes* here.

She frowned.

Hold that thought, Jack said.

He disappeared into the living room and when he came back Claire had opened two new bottles of beer and returned to her spot on the counter, her new beer in hand.

How's this, Jack asked.

It's perfect, Claire said quietly.

It's the mix you made of Dave Matthews and U2, so I figured you would like it, Jack said. Bono was singing One and Claire got far away.

Earth to Claire, Jack whispered.

Claire looked up and into Jack's eyes. His eyes were the color of the deepest blue, so intense and imploring that sometimes Claire had to look away. But she didn't tonight. She looked at him and smiled and he slowly walked to her, cupped her face in his hands, and without a word, leaned in and kissed her.

Claire was surprised, not that Jack was kissing her, but surprised that she wasn't doing anything to stop it. She was always so cognizant of their age difference and always wanted to be appropriate, never wanting to give mixed signals. But here she was, kissing him back, feeling his hands go from holding her face to holding her head, to grasping her hair, and the smallest of moans escaped her mouth.

Jack pulled back ever so slightly and looked her in the eyes. Claire, this is cool, right? She bit her lower lip slightly and looked at him with total concentration. Her smile was all he needed as approval. With that, he scooped her off the kitchen countered and carried her into his bedroom and gently laid her down on the tan and navy comforter. He sat next to her and leaned down, kissing her gently. He unbuttoned her black sweater to expose her black lace bra and ran his hands along her body. He slipped off her heels and ran his fingers along her smooth bare legs. They stared at each other in anticipation. Dave Matthews was singing about satellites. Claire was certain that she was really wet and Jack confirmed that as his hand made its way up her leg, pushing her skirt up and with one finger, hooking her panties so that they coiled back as if in concession. He slid his finger inside her and now it was his turn to let out a moan. For the second time that night Claire heard him say, Nice, Claire.

He pulled her panties off and pushed her skirt up more, licked his finger, leaned in and kissed Claire deeply, sincerely, and Claire felt like she wanted to take care of him forever. He pulled away slightly, kissed her forehand, and put his hand back to where she was hot and wet. Claire, Jack said quietly, you are so beautiful. Just relax, ok? I just want to make you feel good. He put his arm around her shoulders and stroked her hair. He looked in her eyes and she could feel his breath on her face as he gently rubbed in circles, his hands getting soaked and his penis growing harder, pushing up against her leg. She nodded, because it was all she could do. She wanted to do so many things, kiss him, feel him closer to her body, feel him on top of her, pull off his pants and feel his skin, but she couldn't move, except to meet his fingers that were controlling every motion of her body. Jack was touching her in the tiniest of circles in what seemed like the slowest of motions. There was a point where it became almost unbearable, when Claire felt like she was going to jump up, rip off his clothes, and get on top of him. But she didn't; she couldn't. And suddenly there came a moment when everything became far away, when all she could hear was John Legend singing about Ordinary People and her legs got tight and her back arched and Jack leaned in and kissed her and continued to gently wrap her hair in his fingers, and he continued to slowly rub in the tiniest of circles, until Claire lost control and came. Jack was holding her closely, whispering something about having to go now, and she was confused.

Claire opened her eyes only to find that she was alone and had just had the most sexually explosive dream she could recall in a long time. She looked at the clock and sighed. Man, she said out loud. Her covers were twisted, she was twisted, and the alarm decided to make it official: time to get up, Claire.

Chapter 41

Albert Palletti went to his niece's house for Thanksgiving. He hated it there, because he felt like an outsider. He had a large family of course, and he was always invited to a sister's or brother's house, or now, as they got older, a niece's or nephew's. But he was always the lone person, no wife, no kids, he felt as though when someone called to invite him, they would inevitably get off the phone and say to their significant other, sighing sadly, I just spoke with Albert. He'll be coming this year. I feel so bad for that poor man. He felt like he could dissolve into the ground at family functions and no one would even notice. If I died tomorrow, he thought, I wonder what people would say about me. Albert Palletti was a good mailman, he thought to himself. Ha, if they only knew.

Claire went to her friend Jessica's aunt's house. Initially she was hesitant, but she knew that Alex would also be there, and Jessica's husband Justin, and his sister Elizabeth, and Charlie too. A great group of friends, and so she went and ended up having a great time. Thanksgiving was Claire's favorite holiday because she felt like it was meaningful, giving thanks for what you have in life, and being able to share it with the people that matter to you. She felt hollow at the thought of another year in which she was not in a relationship. She wanted to feel connected to someone, and yet, she knew it was something that wouldn't just be handed to her. She pictured Ed McMahon ringing her doorbell, people surrounding him with dozens of balloons, a long, antiquated microphone in front of him. Claire Cassidy, he would yell. Yes, she would say, I'm Claire Cassidy. Well Claire, Ed would respond enthusiastically, You just won a meaningful connection with happiness guaranteed for the rest of your life!

Hey Claire, do you want a glass of wine? Charlie startled her from her ridiculous daydream.

She laughed. Um, yes please, that would be great.

Wherever you were Claire, I hope it was good. Charlie smiled and winked at her. Red, I assume.

Yes please. I was just thinking about Ed McMahon, she started and then paused. Yeah, that sounds weird so let's just not bother. I can't wait to try your homemade apple pie she said, hugging Charlie from behind. It was probably the seventh time that day that Claire silently thanked God for her wonderful friends.

Adam Foster went to a colleague's house. Amy had moved out over a year ago, so it was technically his second round of Major Holidays without her. Her family was all local, so they had spent most Thanksgivings at her parents' house in Madison. Last year, he went home to Maine to be with his family, and it served him well to be surrounded by people who cared about him. Walking in on Amy months beforehand with some neurologist at Yale had sent him into a tailspin. This year though, he was doing much better, and didn't feel like he needed to get back home for both Thanksgiving and Christmas. He had the dogs, he had his friends, he had a stack of books to get through, and he was looking forward to a few good cups of coffee at Café Atlantique over the long Thanksgiving weekend.

Claire went home that night and before she went to bed, she gave thanks aloud: I am grateful for my health, my friends, my family, and I am thankful that I am not in an unhappy relationship. I am hopeful that eventually I will find the right person, but right now I am thankful for the strength I have to live truly and authentically and if that means being alone for now, that's ok.

Adam Foster went home and let the dogs, Alobar and Kudra, out. He named the dogs after the main characters in one of his favorite books, Jitterbug Perfume, by Tom Robbins. As a literature professor at Yale, this was an unusual favorite, since everyone assumed that the classics were his favorites, and his dogs should be named Othello and Macbeth, or Romeo and Juliet. But Adam liked the story of Alobar and Kudra, he liked the timelessness of their relationship and how they had found the key to longevity. He pondered that for a moment while he stood on his back porch and looked at the star-lit sky. I am in a good place, he said aloud. I may be alone, but I am truer than I have ever been, and I am so lucky to have a great family, a great job, close friends and my wonderful dogs. Thank you, he said quietly to the universe.

Albert Palletti did not give thanks to anyone or anything. In fact, he felt quite ill.

Chapter 42

Claire went to bed hoping that she wouldn't have any sexual dreams about Jack again. She thought about her plans for the following day: an early morning bike ride, breakfast with Alex, a little pottery painting, and then she thought she might like to go up to Café Atlantique and write for a little while. Claire liked to write around the holidays. Maybe it was more accurate to say she *felt compelled* to write. She realized that it was more a "year in review" than anything else. She liked doing it over a cup of coffee, which could sometimes progress to a glass of wine. Or two, depending. She could go months without writing a single word about her thoughts or feelings, but then when she sat down to do so, her pen wouldn't be able to keep up with her brain. She started thinking illogical thoughts, about people that she worked with being in a circus, and she realized that it was that weird time where you just start to fall asleep but before you do, you have to have some wacky thoughts. She smiled and fell asleep.

Chapter 43

Claire called Alex and invited her over for breakfast. Why don't you come here, I want to make us breakfast.

Alex said, Really? But I want pancakes and bacon and hash browns.

Good, Claire said, That's fine.

Alright, Alex said. Did you already go for your ride?

Yes, Claire said. I've been up since 5.

Come again, said Alex, WTF, sister?

Oh, I just got enough sleep, that's all, said Claire. So give me an hour and come over, I'll get the stuff for breakfast.

Right on, Claire, I don't know where you find the energy, Alex said, laughing. See you around 11:30.

When Alex arrived, Claire had made a feast. Is anyone else coming, Alex joked.

I know, I made a lot of food, Claire laughed, a bit nervously.

Halfway through breakfast, the oven timer went off and Claire got up. She pulled some white chocolate brownies out of the oven, and Alex stopped chewing for a minute. Oh Claire, she said, now I get it, all the food. The breakfast just kinda threw me, but now that I see the brownies . . . you had a dream about Douglas again, didn't you?

Claire burned herself on the pan. Fuck me, she exclaimed, and then immediately apologized. Yes, I did, she said.

Thousands of miles away, Douglas Bach burned his mouth on the steaming hot cup of coffee he was drinking and said the exact same thing.

Chapter 44

Albert Palletti continued to feel like crap for days following the holiday. It must have been that shitty food that Jackie made, he thought. All that gravy, it can't be good for you. He contemplated this over his ham egg and cheese crepe at Café Atlantique. He felt even worse when he saw that girl come in and hug the waitress behind the counter. Oh, of course the girl with the bright blue eyes that smiles at me is just so friendly that even the staff like her. Bitch. I bet she's a lawyer.

Claire looked over at Albert, and for a moment, he wondered if maybe she had the talent of reading minds. Or maybe my thinking compelled her to look my way. She smiled at him and walked towards him. She also wondered something: I wonder what it is about this greasy looking dude that makes me feel connected to him. Then she noticed his jacket: He was wearing his US Postal Service jacket, and Claire wondered if maybe at some point he had been her mailman, and she had just stored his face away somewhere along the way. I bet that's what it is, she thought, happy with herself for finally [maybe] figuring it out. When he left the café and they made eye contact, she smiled and sang, Wait a minute, Mr. Postman! He looked dumbfounded.

Sorry, Claire said, I bet you hear that all the time.

Not really, Albert said, startled, and he walked out into the street, confused, lonely, tired, and empty. No one ever really spoke much to him, he thought, and that felt painful to him. But he had other things to consider. As he approached his car, he suddenly felt an unbearable pain in his chest, one that defied any adjectives, a blinding pain that was out of this world, and as he clutched his chest, he dropped to his knees and hoped that no one could see him. Is this what it feels like to die, he wondered, as he had a heart attack just outside of the Milford train station. His heart stopped beating at 4:47pm and he was pronounced dead as soon as he reached Milford Hospital.

Chapter 45

Claire in Milford and Douglas in Montana didn't even flinch when Albert Palletti died.

Chapter 46

Claire sat at Café Atlantique, writing happily. She had consumed a large decaf caramel latte and suddenly realized that two hours had evaporated. She went up to the counter and contemplated the wine selection. She didn't notice Adam Foster, aka Handsome Guy, sitting at the table behind her. I haven't had this Chianti before, she said to Elena, the girl at the counter. Do you know if it's any good?

Elena smiled and said, I'm sorry Claire, I haven't tried this yet.

It's good, a voice said from behind her. She turned, and there was Handsome Guy. She smiled at him. It is, huh? she replied. Yes, he said in a quiet and somewhat embarrassed way. Claire turned back to Elena and they exchanged a giddy schoolgirl sort of look.

Alright Elena, I'll try the Chianti.

Claire took a sip and turned to look at Handsome Guy. She felt light and airy and a little self-conscious. It's delicious, she said. Thanks for the recommendation.

Oh, you're welcome, he said, in a way that made her feel that he was just as airy and self-conscious as she was.

I feel like we keep running into each other, she said, I'm Claire. She held out her hand.

Hi Claire, I'm Adam, he said, as he took her hand. Yes, it does seem as though we see each other here quite a bit. It's nice to meet you.

She was about to say, Define 'here' since she had been referring to this place, as well as CVS and Stop&Shop. But she didn't. She just smiled and nodded.

Well, I didn't mean to interrupt your book, she said, and looked at it as she made the comment. Oh wow, Blindess? Jose Saramago? I love that book, she said, way too enthusiastically. Oh man, I must sound like such a dork. I just really like books. Yikes, I'm making it worse. "I love books" she mimicked herself.

Adam could barely contain himself. She knows who Jose Saramago is, wow, and she has read this. Wow. It was really all Adam could think: wow.

There are passages from that book that I cannot forget, Claire admitted. I read it in . . . 1999 or 2000. It's amazing. He's an incredible writer.

Who's your favorite author, Adam asked.

Oh my, that's a tough question, Claire said. I really like Ayn Rand and Richard Bach. I read a lot of different things. These days, I find myself spending hours at Borders buying books that just look good to me. She rolled her eyes and admitted again: I guess I'm kind of a book nerd.

How about you, she asked, and she felt daring just asking this simple question. Elena was watching the exchange and smiling, Claire could see from the corner of her eye.

Well, he said, I'm a literature professor at a local university. So I read a lot. I like Ayn Rand very much. Interesting philosophy. It makes for very intense discussions with my students. My favorite author is probably Leo Tolstoy. I also really admire Milan Kundera.

Well, Claire said, I must be such a novice compared to you. The only Tolstoy I've read is Anna Karenina. I loved it. She leaned in toward him, against the table. It was an incredible story. I remember reading it on the train when I lived in DC. The part where she jumped in front of the train—I was actually on the metro at the time. And even though I knew that she was going to kill herself—in fact, even though I knew she was going to kill herself by jumping in front of a train—I was still completely startled. That's true talent, Claire said, transported to herself of 13 years ago when she sat and read that book on the metro. The orange line. New Carrollton to Macpherson Square.

Sorry, she said, I was just totally back there when I was reading that book. She scrunched up her nose and looked at him with a big, bright smile.

No, please, it's lovely to talk with someone who admires books and feels emotionally attached to them. It's amazing when people get it, when they make the connection to characters.

I agree, said Claire. Did he just use the word 'lovely', she thought to herself.

Are you meeting someone here, he said.

No, I just came up here to write for a little while, Claire replied.

You're a writer? He asked with a smile that said he was happy, but not too surprised.

Well, you know, not really, Claire said in an embarrassed way. I'm no Ayn Rand, she laughed.

He laughed too. Thank goodness, he said.

No, I just write towards the end of the year a lot, kind of the year in review stuff, assessing where I am, where I want to be, how the year was, all that good stuff, she said honestly, feeling a little weird.

So how was 2006 for you, Claire? Adam asked.

Well, Claire said, with a sigh, I am grateful for a lot in my life. I'm really fortunate and I don't take much for granted. She continued, I have realized there are things about myself that I can't change—for example, I analyze the crap out of a lot of things, and I fought that for years. Now that I don't fight it, I worry less about my analyzing. Does that make sense?

Yes, he said, looking at her intensely, but with a smile on his face.

I don't want to take you away from your writing, Adam said, but would you like to have that Chianti with me?

Claire looked down at the Chianti and felt her stomach tremble. That would be nice, she said.

And so it began, the first conversation between Claire and Adam. The spoke about their favorite books and wine, about where they lived in Milford and about Thanksgiving. Claire learned that Adam spent the holiday with the family of a friend slash colleague, and Adam learned that Claire had a very small family that lived out of state. They had similar taste in music, Adam was more forgiving towards rap than Claire, but he agreed that in principle it was hard to say "Fiddy Cent" rather than "Fifty Cents." Fifty is plural, Claire said emphatically, so I have to say, Cents! With an S, she said, as if she wasn't being quite clear enough.

I understand, Adam laughed, I get it, believe me, I am a literature professor! The flow of words and language mean a great deal to me, and grammar is an integral part of that. It's maddening when people use things like—and they said in unison, Double negatives! They laughed and Elena walked over with two new glasses of Chianti. It's on the house, Elena said, and smiled her big cantaloupe smile. She was so warm and earthy and genuine. And if she had filled the glasses anymore they would have been overflowing.

Elena, that's so kind of you, Claire said, as Elena walked away. She wasn't interested in getting in on the conversation, she just wanted Claire and Adam to stay and talk.

And they did. They finished their first glass of wine, then drank the second one courtesy of Elena. It was getting late and Claire asked Adam his last name, in a giddy way, with her hand supporting her face, looking into his face as if he had just told her a big secret. Foster, he replied, staring back at her in a similar fashion, both of them feeling the slightest effect of the wine.

Well, Professor Foster, do you have any classes tomorrow?

No, Claire, this is winter break, so I have no classes.

Lucky! She said, in her Napoleon Dynamite voice. And she felt instantly self-conscious. But it was completely unnecessary, because Adam laughed and replied "God!" in his own version of Napoleon Dynamite. Wow, they both thought, as they looked at each other and laughed.

Well, Adam, I'm jealous. I hope you'll do something fun during your break.

I'll see my family around Christmastime. They live up in Massachusetts. I mentioned that already, didn't I, he said sheepishly.

Yes, Claire said with a smile. Don't worry, Elena gave us enormous glasses of wine. Besides, repetition is good, she said. Makes us remember things.

Have I mentioned that I've really enjoyed spending some time talking with you, Adam asked.

You have, she replied, with a face that could only be described as beaming.

Good, he said, with a warmth and sincerity that made Claire feel vulnerable, but in a good way.Remember that.

Claire, Adam said, I know you don't really know me, but you did tell me were you live, so can I drive you home? It's dark and I would just feel better knowing that you got home safely. Or I could walk you home. Is that ok?

Claire hesitated a little, a chunk of caution that she carried with her always. Um, she said, that's very sweet of you. I think I feel ok with you driving me home. I feel bad about you walking me home, because then you'll be walking alone in the dark, she said.

Well, but I'm a guy, Adam started, but he stopped and just smiled. He helped Claire with her coat and together they waved goodbye to Elena. Goodnight, Elena, Claire said, and thanks for the wines. Elena tilted her head and sang, Bye Guys! Claire winked at her as she turned to leave.

Adam Foster drove Claire home in his Volvo wagon, which he explained was a necessity for his two dogs.

You have dogs! Claire squealed in excitement, and then said, Oh geez, I'm sorry, that was crazy how excited I just got about you having dogs. That must have been creepy.

He laughed. No Claire, clowns are creepy. You are cute, he said, and he touched her hand that was sitting on her lap.

What kind of dogs are they? She inquired in a more tempered tone.

Vizlas, he replied. They're reddish, about mid-size—Claire stopped him. I know what kind of dogs they are, she said quietly, her heart in her throat. They're one of my favorites. I've wanted one for a while. They have such nice demeanors.

Yes! Adam said, and he laughed at his own excitement. Ok, he said, now I just acted way too happy—we're even.

Claire smiled but she was a little weirded out. They'd had a great conversation, he was smart and nice and funny and he had the kind of dogs that she wanted. Oh yeah, and he drove a Volvo wagon, her internal voice reminded her.

What are their names, Claire asked timidly, hoping that he wouldn't take his hand off of hers. It had been there for about a minute now and he was starting to gently rub his thumb back and forth over her skin.

Oh, ok, he said, they're kind of weird names, he said. One of my favorite couples from one of my favorite books. Alobar and Kudra, he said, looking at her with the slightest doubt on his face, as if to say, you can't possibly know who they are, right?

Claire felt overwhelmed and dizzy and she wasn't sure if it was the wine or the experience of this whole afternoon, or the fact that Adam's dogs were named after one of her favorite books too. Her jaw dropped slightly and she looked over at Adam. Jitterbug Perfume, she said quietly.

Wow, they said simultaneously.

Chapter 47

Claire called Alex the next day and told her about meeting Adam.

Wait, is that the cute guy with the Clark Kent glasses that you keep running into? He wears funky shoes?

Yes, Claire said, laughing. He is awesome, she said, and anyone that heard it over the phone would have thought she was seventeen. But you wouldn't know it the way you're describing him Alex, geez! Clark Kent glasses and funky shoes. Sounds like he's in special ed!

Alex laughed, Geez Claire, that's pretty cool, you sound sooooooooooo happy.

Well, Claire said, I have to have realistic expectations—

Ugh Claire, for the love of God, just be happy! Alex yelled playfully.

Ok, Claire said, laughing back. It was fun. He's just so . . . lovely, she said. OH! And he used the word 'lovely'—you know how you are always making fun of me because I say lovely??

Wait a minute, missy, Alex interjected. Did you just say *always*?

They giggled until Claire had to get off the phone because her boss was opening his door and she didn't want to sound too happy too early in the morning. She didn't like him knowing about her personal life, the conversations just felt too contrived.

But Alex called back two minutes later. Girlfriend, she said to Claire, how the hell did you leave it with him?

Oh, Claire said, and smiled. We're going to have dinner on Friday night. And hopefully we'll talk before that.

Ok, right on, said Alex. Have a great day.

You too, said Claire. And so it was early on this particular day that she thanked the universe before 8am for having wonderful friends.

Chapter 48

Roberta Angellino made arrangements for her brother's funeral. She wasn't sure if she should have him cremated. He didn't have a plot and it was expensive to buy one. And caskets were so expensive too she thought, Good Lord! All for a box of wood that's going to sit in the ground and be eaten up by worms and maggots. She stopped herself because she knew there was no way she wanted to be cremated.

Albert never discussed what he wanted with his family, she said. He was a quiet man, and even more so after his wife left him, even though that was over twenty years ago. Roberta thought about her brother and the only emotion that could be assigned a name was pity. She felt pity for him. He never had the life he wanted, she thought, and yet, he didn't do much to change things, either. He was a passive character in his own game of Life. She shook her head and said sadly, Albert, you poor thing.

When she returned home, she called Jackie, her daughter, Albert's niece, the one who had hosted Thanksgiving. Roberta sighed heavily and said, Well Jack, I decided to have your uncle cremated. I know it might sound awful, but caskets are really expensive and he didn't leave any instructions or wishes about how he wanted to be buried.

Ma, don't beat yourself up, Jackie said. She was holding her 2 year old daughter, Caitlin, on her hip, and stirring sauce with the other hand. Uncle Albert was a loner and a sad man. I feel bad for him, and I hate to say this, but he's probably better off. What kind of life did he have, Ma? Delivering mail and eating frozen dinners. Fuck that shit.

Do you kiss your daughter with that mouth, Roberta asked in feigned disgust.

Sorry Ma, it's just sad is all, and I feel bad that you have to take care of all of it. You always gotta take care of the sh—crap in this family.

I know, Roberta said, glad that someone recognized it.

Well, he's being cremated tomorrow, and I'll get the ashes, maybe we can think about where we can scatter them, somewhere nice for your Uncle Albert. I'm not going to do a wake because he didn't really have any friends, just us family. We'll have a nice Catholic ceremony for him though. It'll be small. Do you think I should buy one of those big wreaths of flowers, you know, the ones that look like a horseshoe?

No Ma, just make it simple. Flowers are a waste of money, anyway. They'll just die.

Those words lingered between them in awkward silence for a moment and then it passed and Roberta said, Ok hon, I'll let you know how things go, I have to write this obituary I guess, I don't know what the hell I'm going to say. Poor Uncle Albert, was what she said. I'll talk to you tomorrow.

Chapter 49

It wasn't because I just met a nice guy, Claire reasoned. She sat in her car and watched the waves crash into the shore, listening to Crash Into Me. What a coincidence, she thought, until she reminded herself that coincidences are just events that need special attention. Or rather, that being open to things that seemed coincidental opened your mind to many new things. Then she shook her head and wondered if she had ADD, because sometimes her head wouldn't let her concentrate on one thought. She went back to it: it's not because I just met someone. He may never call me, or he may turn out to be a freak. God knows I have met my share of freaks in the last couple of years. Anyway. This is not about anyone but me.

Douglas, she said out loud, it's time for me to let go. I've carried you in my heart for years. I've carried this letter with me for months. I know I could try to find you if I wanted to. Maybe someday I will. Right now, I still can't. So, here it is. My letter to you. I feel like a dork, but I have stuffed it in a bottle. Not just any bottle though, she laughed. An empty bottle of Cakebread Merlot. It was delicious, she said, smiling. I just didn't want to keep the letter. I didn't want to ask any friends to hold it for me, and I didn't want to give it to Patty Blake. I figured this is the most cliché way to get rid of it. But, Douglas, I don't expect it to make its way to you. I have no expectations of goofy, cheesy, unrealistic romantic endings.

She got out of the car and walked to the water. In fact, she continued, I hope no one finds this, unless they are in like, Papua New Guinea, and they don't give a rat's ass about some stupid letter in a former bottle of wine. And with that, she walked as far out on the breakers as she could, and gently placed the bottle in the water, and watched it float away, until she wasn't sure if she could see it anymore, or if her eyes were playing tricks on her. Bye Douglas, I hope you are happy and healthy, she whispered.

Claire headed back to her car and turned on the heat. It was a mild winter so far but still, she was chilled. She sat for a while and listened to Substitute for Love by Madonna, and remembered listening to the song once when she was married, on her way home from work. It was a dark, cold winter night and she recalled feeling so depleted by pretending to be happy. She had wondered at that time if she would ever feel settled without feeling like she had settled.

Chapter 50

Claire and Adam had exchanged phone numbers and email addresses that night at the coffee shop, and indeed, Adam had emailed her the following evening to say what a pleasure it was to meet her. His email made her smile:

> *Hi Claire, good morning. I hope your day is going well. I just wanted to tell you that I had a really nice time talking with you yesterday. It was a genuine pleasure. I'm still a little freaked out about the dogs. Not many people know who Alobar and Kudra are. I guess it just goes to show that we should always be open to the small surprises that are often right in front of us . . . if only we look.*
>
> *Have a good day, and I'll connect with you before Friday to confirm plans.*
>
> *Adam*

Claire was cautiously excited. She didn't want to have high expectations, because she didn't want to be let down. She thought of Jim and how excited she had been about him—and they had had six dates! How many dates do I need to have with someone to know, she asked Danielle one afternoon in the cafeteria over lunch.

Danielle's eyes grew large and she looked at Claire as if to say, Are you really asking me that? Claire had given her the low-down about Adam over their salads. Claire, Danielle said, you are an adult. You have had some serious trust issues. Your husband cheated on you and never made you a priority in his life. Your first love took off and left you with a sense of abandonment that has stuck with you. But you have come a long way. You're a smart woman and you are so logical. You know all the answers

Claire, all the answers that you need, anyway. Remember that saying, the answers already lie within us? I think in your heart you really do know that.

I love when you get all deep on me, Danielle, Claire said, only half-joking. They smiled. I know I'm ok, Claire said softly. I don't even really know this guy, but I actually feel good and I feel like maybe that trip to Copenhagen helped me clear out my head. I know I'm not a perfect person, but man, I am honest and sincere, funny . . . and I can bake a mean cookie.

They laughed. Danielle looked at Claire and said, I think you're fine. I think you're better than fine. I think you have found inside you that you are fine, good, GREAT even! You know who you are. Some people never really know themselves. So just be you and have fun with this guy. And of course, email me over the weekend to let me know how it goes!

I will, Claire said. Tell me about your Thanksgiving, she said. How did your mom's visit go?

Danielle rolled her eyes and sighed, and they spent the remainder of their lunch discussing the sensitivities of familial relationships.

Chapter 51

Claire had been seeing Adam for three weeks. Their first dinner had been as comfortable as could be, with the exception of the trembling in her tummy for the first hour. He just made her feel so relaxed though, and apparently she had the same effect on him. They went to Barcelona in Fairfield and shared some yummy tapas: roasted chickpea puree, eggplant jam, artichoke hearts, roasted asparagus, and tuna with pistachios and leeks. They laughed over delicious sangria about the weird combinations, and they concluded that the person that came up with this stuff was either high or drunk but brilliant nonetheless. That date was light and fluffy, no heavy discussions, just work, books, dogs, and somehow the topic of working out came up, shockingly. When Adam had brought Claire home that night, he said simply, Claire, I really enjoy you. Thanks for spending the evening with me. I hope you'll want to do it again soon. Yes, she had replied, I would really like that. He had kissed her cheek softly and walked her to her door. When he drove away, she walked up the stairs to her apartment, thinking about how soft his lips were, wondering what it would be like to kiss them.

She found out. Their next date was a trip to the British Art Museum in New Haven followed by dinner at Roomba. When they left Roomba, they walked all around New Haven—up Chapel Street, down Crown Street, over to Whalley and back around to Yale. Adam knew New Haven; he taught there, at Yale. She had learned that on their first date. A Yale professor, oh man, she had thought, and then she stopped herself. Don't, Claire, don't. They had already talked for hours, and this time the subject matter had been decidedly more intimate than that fun night at Barcelona.

Over dinner, Adam explained his "failed" relationship with Amy, his "college sweetheart" if you will, he had said, rolling his eyes. He said that he should have seen the signs, that they had become "too comfortable" with each other and would spend a lot of time together without saying a word. He realized now that he was a chatterbox at heart and in retrospect, saw how detrimental it was to be in a relationship where he wasn't really connected. He had used the word "connected" and Claire instantly felt that he wanted the same kind of "connection" that she did. He said that he and Amy had grown apart—that as they grew up, they had become different people. Amy was attracted to wealth and prestige, and I should have recognized that sooner, Adam said in a melancholy tone. She grew up in Madison, Connecticut, at yacht clubs with her parents. She went to school never having to worry about paying student loans. She walked around in J Crew and Banana Republic clothes and couldn't even relate to the fact that I was on a budget. Honestly, she just could not relate. Anyway, Adam had said, we were living together when I found out that she was seeing a neurologist at Yale. She had met him at the Starbucks on Chapel Street, the one just a few blocks away from here, he chuckled.

I'm sorry, Claire said, and she put her hand in his and laced their fingers together. He squeezed her fingers and looked at her, smiling a sad smile. I wouldn't dare to say that I understand how you feel, because I'm not you, Claire said. I found out that my husband had been seeing someone too. For me, it was validation that the relationship was over, and now that I knew something definitive, I felt justified in ending the relationship . . ."officially." Sometimes I wish that I had done so sooner, but everything I have done in my life has led me to where I am right now, and . . . I like where I am. He squeezed her fingers again and pulled him toward her. He leaned in and said, I like where you are too, Claire, and he kissed her mouth gently. It wasn't a long kiss, and he pulled away slightly afterwards. But it felt lovely, and so full of intensity, meaning, and understanding, Claire thought.

I hope that was ok, he said.

Yes, it was more than ok, Claire said, biting her lower lip slightly, while telling herself not to bite her lip.

Good. He smiled. I have been wanting to kiss you ever since I saw you that day at Atlantique, when you were with your friend. She tilted her head sideways as if to say, Which time? And Adam laughed. Remember, he said, You guys were discussing my shoes.

It was the perfect way to transition from the heavy conversation. All of it would come out in time, she thought, his losses, my losses, his imperfections, my imperfections, his shining moments and mine. She didn't feel rushed, she didn't feel inadequate, she didn't feel scared. She just felt content.

Oh my God, Adam, she laughed, we *were* talking about your shoes, how did you know??

I have bionic ears, he said, in a serious tone and with a goofy smile. I heard your friend say that she liked my shoes, and you turned around and tried to be smooth, but you were so obvious!

Lyndsay, Claire said. She's so sweet. She's a pastry chef, you know.

I didn't know that, Adam said in mock surprise.

And so they sat there and discussed their friends, and Claire told Adam all about Alex and Danielle, Isabelle and Lyndsay, and Jessica and Justin. He told her about friends from Massachusetts, the ones that he couldn't imagine ever losing touch with, kids he knew all the way back to grade school, and the newer friends down here at Yale, his colleagues and other professors, and he had even made a couple of friends in Milford, since moving there after the split with Amy.

They learned more and more about each other that night. Claire had yet to drop the whole Douglas story on him, but again, she didn't feel like there was a need to rush. Adam was a gentle, kind, understanding guy, and she felt good that they had been able to talk about Amy and Rick, their respective ex-partners, without getting into a lot of detail, and without depleting their energy. Claire hadn't planned on telling him about Rick on Date # 2, but she rationalized, they had spent hours at Café Atlantique that first day, when they shared those huge glasses of Chianti. And then Barcelona, everything there was pretty light, and that date had lasted over four hours. And then she stopped herself and thought, Claire, stop analyzing. Just do what comes naturally, just do what feels right.

He drove her home and they made plans in the car to get together the following evening. They looked at each other funny and Claire said, I know, two dates in two consecutive days. But don't worry, we're just going to see a movie. It's nothing major. She smiled, trying to convince herself as well as Adam.

Darn, Adam joked. He leaned over and brushed the hair out of Claire's eyes. You have such pretty eyes, he said, and his hand lingered in her hair. He twirled her hair around his fingers and Claire felt warm inside. She wasn't ready to invite him in, besides it was late, and she thought it best to leave off on a high note, and not spend too much time in the car so that it would start to get uncomfortable.

I had a great time tonight, said Claire. Thanks again. Some of the subject matter was a little intense for this early on, but I just want you to know that I value honesty more than anything else, and so I'm glad that you were honest and that you felt comfortable enough with me to tell me something so personal.

I do feel comfortable with you, Claire, Adam said, still twirling her hair in his fingers and still looking at her intently. I'm glad that we both seem to appreciate the same things, like honesty and communication. It's really a pleasure getting to know you, he said.

And then there was the awkwardness in the car that Claire didn't want to happen. They had only shared that one kiss at the restaurant that evening, during the intense conversation, but it seemed like a goodnight kiss was appropriate; more than that, it seemed like a goodnight kiss was something they both wanted.

He started to laugh.

What, Claire said, smiling and looking around as though someone was playing a joke on her.

I just think it's kinda neat that we feel weird about the fact that we both want to kiss one another and we're in our 30s. I'm glad that feeling hasn't gone away. I'm glad that I really want to kiss you.

Claire smiled, this time in confirmation. She leaned over the console and touched the side of his face. He moved his face to meet her hand, and brought his hand up and placed it on hers. He gently took her hand away and interlaced their fingers, laying them on his leg. He touched her hair again, Claire's chocolate brown hair, and pulled her toward him. He kissed her softly, his lips touching hers delicately. It seemed to Claire that maybe this felt as amazing to him as it did to her, but she didn't want to make any assumptions. And here I am analyzing this beautiful kiss, she thought, and she made herself stop, and Adam thought, I wonder if she feels like this is as amazing as I do.

It didn't last long, relatively speaking. They both had the feeling that they wanted it to go on longer, but they knew they would see each other tomorrow, and there's always the opportunity to make out at the movies, right? Besides, there's something to be said for anticipation, they both realized.

Chapter 52

Claire awoke with a smile on her face. She had slept peacefully, dreaming about her date with Adam. She would wake up in the middle of the night and think, Oh yeah, that actually happened. She felt just pure, simple happiness. She stretched, looked out the window, and said Brrrr, it's really getting cold out, to no one in particular. I'm gonna have to dress warm tonight, she thought. I wonder what I'll wear.

She laughed at herself for thinking such things at 8am, when they weren't supposed to get together for about 11 hours.

She went to the gym and ran on the treadmill. She had wanted to go for a bike ride but the air was cold and raw. She ran like crazy and it felt effortless and she knew she was running on adrenaline. She blasted her iPod and listened to The Cure, Pete Yorn, Dave Matthews, and U2, thinking about the night ahead.

Adam had called her while she was at the gym and asked if she wanted to go for a hike with him and the dogs. She smiled and said, Uh, yes! to the voicemail. She finished listening to his message, which ended with a "look forward to seeing you" and drove home. She called him while she was still sitting in the parking lot.

Hi Adam, she said, how are you?

Good, Claire, you?

I'm good, she said. I just got your message, I was at the gym.

Cool, he said, did you have a good workout?

I did, Claire replied, thanks. And I'd be happy to take a walk with you and your dogs, she said.

That's great, Adam said.

They made plans to meet in the early afternoon, and then they would bring the dogs home and head out to the movies. They were planning to see *Dan in Real Life*, and grab a coffee afterwards, but now they would be spending the afternoon together and so things would just have to shift slightly. Claire was surprised to find herself strangely comfortable with being spontaneous.

Adam's directions to his house were simple, and they laughed at how close they lived to each other when Claire arrived. When he opened the back door for her, her face was pink. You look cold, Adam said. I am! Claire said, it's getting bitter out.

Ah, December in New England, Adam said sarcastically but in a good natured way.

Exactly, replied Claire. Brrrrrr!

Claire stood in the doorway for a minute feeling awkward. Come in! Adam said, Please. As he said it, Alobar and Kudra rounded the corner and began nudging her with their noses for pets. Hi guys, Claire said, and kneeled down to pet them. They sniffed her and accepted her attention, and Claire was lost in the excitement of playing with the dogs. Until she looked up and saw Adam staring at her and the dogs with a genuine look of contentment on his face. These guys are awesome, Claire said, laughing and smiling.

You are awesome, Adam said, and he took Claire's hand and lifted her up from where she was kneeling, pulled her close to him, pushed her hair from her face and looked in her eyes. You really are, he said, and he kissed her gently. They stood there close to each other, her arms around his waist, and his arms around her shoulders, his hands in her hair. So, Claire said as she leaned into him, should we take these two out for a nice walk?

I suppose, Adam said, Though I feel like I could just stay like this a little longer. He smiled at Claire for a moment and then disentangled himself.

Ally, Kudra, he said loudly in an enthusiastic voice, Wanna go for a ride??

The dogs barked in excitement and ran around them in circles. Claire laughed in delight.

You better bundle up, Adam, it's really getting cold. Do the dogs have sweaters?

Claire, what now? Adam said in shock. Sweaters???

They laughed and got the leashes out and were on their way. Somewhere in New Haven, in the middle of a conversation about hockey, Adam said, Oh my God Claire, I didn't even show you around the house. How rude of me.

That's what I was thinking, Claire said and then looked at him funny. Are you high, she asked. It's ok that you didn't show me around. Besides, I'm guessing we're going back there with the dogs. You can show me around then.

K, Adam replied. And no, I'm not high! He said, poking her stomach playfully.

While they were hiking at Sleeping Giant, the snow started to come down pretty hard. On the decline, they were all cold and wet, Adam, Claire, and the dogs. They got into Adam's silver Volvo wagon and cranked the heat. Claire was shivering and her lower lip quivered.

Oh Claire, you're freezing, Adam said apologetically, rubbing her shoulder. I'm so sorry!

I'm fine, Claire said between quivering lips. Really, I can't stop shivering sometimes, but I'm really ok. I wish I could make my lip stop, she said, embarrassed.

Let me help, Adam said, and he kissed her, this time a little more passionately then the previous kisses. When he pulled away, he smiled. She looked at him for a moment. Your lip stopped, he said.

So it did, Claire said with a smile. Let's get out of here before we're stranded! The snow is coming down like crazy!

The roads were getting bad and they decided on the way back to Adam's that they would not go to the movies tonight, and that Claire would need to stay over for a while until the storm ended. It was supposed to be a quick blizzard and then the temperature was going to rise and melt everything. And so they headed back to Adam's and unloaded the dogs and hurried inside. They removed their snowy shoes and Claire took off her jacket. Her jeans were soaked. Uh-oh, Adam said, you need to change.

Well, Claire said, I don't have a change of clothes, do you have a blow dryer?

Adam laughed. How embarrassing, he said, Yes I do. But I can throw your jeans in the dryer. Do you feel weird wearing a pair of my sweats?

The very thought made her feel warm. Yeah, I think I could handle that, she said.

Good, Adam replied. I'll be right back. But first, he said, come in, please, and sit down. He brought her into the living room, which was comfy and decorated in earthy tones. A big comfortable looking couch, but not one of those crazy contemporary oversized couches. Browns and greens and burgundies filled the room. She felt cozy and relaxed—except for the wet jeans.

Adam went upstairs and while he was there she looked around at the pictures in his living room—pictures of him and his brothers, a photo of Adam with his niece and nephew, a nicely framed photo of the dogs, and one of his parents at a reception of some sort. Adam was so boyishly handsome she thought. And so genuine and unassuming. She felt really good about him. She didn't want to get too excited and yet, she was. They both had a lightnesss to them when they were around each other. Adam returned to the living room and presented Claire with a pair of worn sweats, a t-shirt, a flannel shirt, and a pair of white sport socks. He had already changed into different jeans and a worn-looking sweatshirt, socks and no shoes. He looked comfy and relaxed.

Oh my, Claire said, her eyes opened wide. Thank you.

I know they'll be kinda big, but at least you'll be warm and dry, Adam said.

Um yeah, I'm sure I'll look like a real treat, Claire laughed.

Claire, Adam said, actually I think it'll be pretty cool to see you in my clothes. He wrapped his arm around her and said, Huh, I guess you don't even know where the bathroom is. I am a bad host!

Adam showed Claire to the bathroom and gave her a quick kiss. I'm going to make some coffee he said, to warm us up. Unless you'd prefer tea or hot chocolate?

Coffee sounds great, Claire said.

They sat in Adam's living room with their coffees and talked for hours. The snow had stopped almost as soon as they arrived at Adam's and they heard the drone of the plows in the distance. Claire figured she would leave at some point—maybe before dinner? And then they would see a movie another night. There was no doubt in Claire's mind that she would see Adam again, unlike Jim, when every time they had what seemed like a great date, she would drive away wondering if he was going to call her.

As she was thinking this, Adam said Claire, let's build a fire. I'll go get some wood, ok?

And Claire smiled back at Adam. That sounds great, she said. I'm good at building fires.

You *are*? He said enthusiastically. He got up, leaned over her, and kissed her nose. It was simple sweet, gentle and intimate all rolled into one. It made Claire feel relaxed and comfortable. By the way, Adam said, you look great in my clothes.

She smiled and gave him a look that said, Yeah right, as he walked out to the deck to get wood for the fire. Kudra woke up from her exercise-induced nap and walked over to Claire, gave her hand a lick, and Claire motioned for her to come up on the couch, where she sat and pet her and talked to her. Aren't you pretty, she said. And you're so nice and you have such a cute little personality. Kudra. Yes you do, she continued, as she pet her face and the length of Kudra's body. I really like your dad, Claire said in a whisper.

Claire felt a cold blast, which meant that Adam was coming in from the deck. Man, it is still so raw out there, she thought. Uh Claire, you should come here and look outside. She turned and looked at him. What's the matter, Claire asked as she got up, carefully moving Kudra's paws from her lap so as not to disrupt her too much.

She walked to the door and he followed her, putting his hand on her back. Holy crap, Claire exclaimed.

The snow had resumed with full force. She thought about how much snow had already been on her car when they came back from the park. She looked at the railing on the deck and saw that there must have been at least eight inches of snow. Whoa, she said.

Yeah I know, said Adam. Yikes.

Well, Adam said, it's 8 o'clock. It's dark and cold and I'm kinda getting hungry. Claire, I don't think that you should drive home in this, I just wouldn't feel comfortable. I know this might feel weird but, why don't you stay over tonight. We can have some dinner and watch a movie and you can stay in the guest room, I'm not suggesting anything other than I don't want you to drive tonight. We can make it a fun night, he said, smiling at her. I think the snow gods are trying to tell us something.

Claire sat there for a minute looking out at the snow, thinking about snow gods. Claire, you're 36. What's the big deal. You trust Adam enough, and you really like him. And he's not some horndog asking you to spend the night with him. He's sincere and concerned about you driving. Just say yes, she thought, just say yes, and before she knew it she heard herself say, Yes, ok, I'll stay. Thanks, Adam.

Cool, he said. Maybe we can go for a walk, too, he said happily. The dogs love the snow.

She smiled back in agreement. I love walking in the snow, everything is so quiet, like there's a layer of insulation around the world.

I like the way you think, Claire, he said. Why don't we make some dinner and then see what the weather is like, and maybe take a nighttime stroll?

Ok, Claire said, but first I just want to call Alex and let her know that I'm ok and I'm spending the night with you.

They looked at each other.

You know what I mean, she exclaimed. He laughed. Actually, I think it's pretty cool that you are so close with your friends.

Well, we're always there for each other. And I think I have already explained to you that I seldom use the words *always* and *never*. My friends support me and I support them. They have kept me going in some crappy times. I know, Adam said, and he put his arms around Claire and hugged her. He said quietly, I know you went through a lot with your divorce, and I can relate to some of it. Lying and deception are hard to swallow. She let herself be hugged by Adam. They sure are, she said.

He pulled back slightly to see her face. And the whole thing about having kids . . . Claire, I know I am probably biased, but that guy didn't deserve you. She made a funny face. Thanks, she said.

They had just talked about it last night and her head was still sorta whirling. They remained wrapped up in each other for another minute or two, until Adam said, Hey Claire, how about some dinner? To which Claire replied quietly, Totally. He kissed her forehead sweetly and took her hand and led her to the kitchen.

Adam fed the dogs and said, Feel free to look around, I'm not really sure what I have in the house. Claire felt awkward at first, looking in the fridge, it's like looking in someone's medicine cabinet, she thought, private insights into people that you don't often have. It feels slightly voyeuristic, she was telling herself, as she pulled a butternut squash, chicken broth, an onion, celery, and half&half from the fridge. Do you like butternut squash soup, she asked.

Uh, yeah, Adam said, Sure I do. But um, I don't think—he looked at Claire, with her hands full from the fridge and stopped mid-sentence.

You have everything we need, she said. I just figured you bought the stuff to make it.

He laughed heartily. That's rich, Claire, he said. No, I'm not exactly a culinary whiz.

How about some salad with the soup, she asked.

Ok, Adam said, what can I do?

Sit there and look pretty, she joked. No, come here, you can cut this squash for me, it's too hard for a girl like me.

Yeah right, Adam said.

And so they made dinner together and while the soup was cooking they looked outside and talked about snowstorms. Do you remember the winter of 93, when it snowed like every other day, Claire asked. Oh man, Adam replied, yes. I was in school and had to walk everywhere in the snow. It was miserable. Thank goodness for my LL Bean boots, he said. Hey, I should be in one of their commercials!

Claire replied back matter-of-factly, LL Bean doesn't do any DTC advertising. Adam laughed. Sorry, Claire said, Work mode. I know, he said, It's cute, and he hugged her from behind.

After dinner they cleaned up and decided against a walk in the snow. It was still coming down hard, only sideways now, and the wind was howling. They decided instead to make the fire they had discussed earlier, and sit and watch a movie. Since it was close to Christmas, Adam said, Hey Claire, do you think it would be lame if we watched It's A Wonderful Life?

Lame? she said in disbelief. Not at all, I think it would be awesome to watch that with you.

I just like to watch it every year, it makes me feel good. It's such a great story, Adam said.

Claire replied, It makes me appreciate and feel good about life, just in general. It's nice to meet someone who appreciates it too.

He looked at her for a minute. Gee Claire, he said slowly, you and I kinda seem to connect on a lot of things.

She smiled. Yup, she said, staring at him. I know.

It was a lovely night they agreed, and they watched It's A Wonderful Life as the fire crackled in the fireplace and the dogs slept on their little LL Bean beds. Adam sat on the couch with his feet on the coffee table, while Claire laid on the couch with her head resting on Adam's leg. He stroked her hair and occasionally rested his hand on the curve of her waist. At one point he pulled back his flannel shirt she was wearing and gently stroked her skin. To Claire, every touch felt electric and yet, like home.

It was close to 11 when the movie ended. They sat on the couch and talked until 2, about their childhoods, their families, books, music, and their former relationships. When they both yawned simultaneously, they looked at each other, smiled, and nodded. Yeah, let's get some sleep, Claire said in a tired voice. Ok, Adam said. He let the dogs out on the deck, where they walked awkwardly through the thick snow to take care of business. Claire and Adam stood at the door watching Alobar and Kudra, giggling like kids over how funny it looked. Poor guys, she said.

Please, Adam said, they love it!

And when the dogs were settled, Adam walked Claire to the guest bedroom and gave her a towel, washcloth, and a new toothbrush (you're lucky, he had said, I just bought a new one last week). They lingered in the doorway, and Adam interlaced his fingers in hers. He turned to look at Claire and kissed her for a long time. Their fingers fell apart and he was holding her face with both of his hands, and soon she was pressed up against the door where they continued to kiss in a way that Claire felt certain she could spend a very long time. But since you can't kiss someone forever, they eventually stopped and put their heads together, so that their foreheads were touching and they could each feel one another breathing.

It's very cool getting to know you Claire, Adam whispered. I really like you.

Claire beamed. I really like you too Adam, she said quietly.

I hope you sleep well, he said, Sweet dreams.

Sweet dreams to you too, Adam. I had a great day with you, and thanks for caring about me enough to have me stay over and not drive, Claire said.

Adam said, I do care, Claire. Goodnight. I'll see you in the morning.

Claire went to bed that night in Adam's guest room thinking, Oh man, he'll see me in the morning, great. But that thought floated in and out of her mind quickly, because she actually didn't care all that much.

And she needn't have cared. They awoke around the same time and took the dogs for a long walk, which included a stop at Dunkin Donuts, where they got coffee and bagels to go. They went back to Adam's, had breakfast, and then Claire changed back into her clothes upstairs. When she came back downstairs, Adam had cleared all of the snow off her car. You are way too nice, she said, Thank you, Adam.

Don't be freaked out Claire, but I kinda wish you didn't have to go, said Adam sheepishly.

Yeah, I know what you mean, Claire said, looking down at her shoes.

Hey Claire, I am going to see my family for Christmas, and I'm leaving on Sunday. Do you think maybe we could get together before then, like Friday or Saturday night?

Of course, Claire said, I would really like that.

Good. Be careful driving home, ok? And I'll talk with you later on?

Yes, and yes, I'll be careful. Thanks again, Claire said.
The pleasure was really all mine, Adam said in a heartfelt way.
Bye, Adam.
Bye, Claire.
When Claire got home, there was a message from her doctor's office confirming her appointment next week, a message from her mom, asking about the snowstorm, and a message from the Postmaster General of Milford, Bob Something-or-Other, asking her to call his office at her earliest convenience. He sounded distressed, and she wondered what that could possibly be about.

Chapter 53

Isabelle left a voicemail for Claire that afternoon, while Claire was at the gym. She needed to talk. Claire called her when she left the gym and asked, Isabelle, are you ok?

Eh, I've been better, Claire, she replied.

They met at Claire's. She made hot tea and they sat on the couch and talked. Isabelle said she was upset because the new guy didn't really work out. He turned out to be kinda weird, Isabelle explained, but when Claire asked in what way, Isabelle just fumbled over her words and made generalizations. Claire took the tea out of Isabelle's hands and placed it down on the table. She hugged her and said, Bella, I worry about you.

Isabelle wanted to cry. She wanted to tell Claire that she had just sent a letter to the man she loved, a letter that said goodbye. Instead, she sucked it up and, as Claire would often say, she pasted on a smile. Claire looked at her. Do you want to say something, Claire asked. Nah, Isabelle said, I'm fine, really. Please, she said, just tell me about Adam. You sound smitten, Claire.

When Isabelle left an hour later, Claire shut the door and it occurred to her that everyone has sides that they just cannot share. She knew that Isabelle was keeping something locked away, and she hoped that she could handle it. God, please let Isabelle be ok, and please let her know that she can talk to me if and when she is ready.

Claire called Alex and asked her if she thought Isabelle was ok. She told her about the strange call she had gotten from Isabelle, and then their visit, and she just felt like something wasn't right.

Huh, Alex said. I'll call her. Check in. Plus, we need to confirm our plans for Christmas. Is Adam going to be around?

No, Claire said, he's going up to Massachusetts to see his family. It's cool, she heard herself saying, We haven't been dating long at all. He's really great though, Alex.

I know, sister, Alex said, I can hear it in your voice. And I know you haven't been dating long but you can tell when there's something there. This is totally different from Jim.

Claire allowed herself to think of Jim. Yeah, she agreed, Something wasn't right there.

Something wasn't right there because something is right *now*, Alex said convincingly. You couldn't have been open to meeting Adam if you were dating Jim. Claire said, I guess you're right, Alex.

Funny how that shit all works out, huh Clairabelle? Alex said matter-of-factly. Like you and your "there are no coincidences" philosophy.

Claire smiled and said, Yes, Alex!

Alex responded, See? I listen.

Chapter 54

Claire met with Patty Blake after work on Wednesday, and she was feeling light and happy and good about everything. She was thinking, as she put her keys on the kitchen counter and played her phone messages, *You either feel totally drained and spent after therapy, or on top of the world.*

There was another voicemail from that Postmaster guy. This time she caught his name: Bob Kimer. He sounded uneasy and stumbled with the message. I'm sorry to be calling again, he said, But I just need to confirm your current address, and I'm wondering if you are the Claire Cassidy that lived in Branford, Connecticut on Hillside Avenue.

What the F, Claire said to herself. She thought, IRS? Lost income tax form? DMV? Long lost creditor? Ugh, she said aloud.

She was jotting down his number when Adam called and asked if she wanted to meet at Café Atlantique for coffee the following evening. She smiled. That would be great, she said, mindlessly putting Bob Kimer's phone number into her bag. They talked for over an hour and by the time she hung up the phone she had forgotten all about the Milford Postmaster General and his weird message.

On Thursday morning, Claire was telling her friend Ann at work that she had a date with Adam that night, just casual, going for coffee at the local coffee shop, and it triggered her memory of the postman guy. She told Ann about it and Ann said, Crap, Claire, that sounds strange.

When you control the mail, you control *information*, Claire said, quoting a Seinfeld episode. I guess I should call this blockhead, she said.

She called and left a message for Bob Kimer: Hi Mr. Kimer, this is Claire Cassidy. I'm returning your call. My current address is Bayview

Avenue in Milford, and yes, I am the Claire Cassidy who lived at Hillside Avenue in Branford, Connecticut. Please call me back; I'm intrigued.

Claire and Adam met at Café Atlantique that night and they talked about their days. She felt funny, like they were a comfortable couple, talking about what they had done that day. The daily minutiae. She liked it. They were happy and relaxed around each other and Claire had almost forgotten to tell him about the odd phone calls she was getting from the Postmaster.

Sounds crazy, huh? She said.

It does sound odd, but I bet it's nothing, Adam said. They probably just need to verify something, or wait! I know! Maybe you won the Publisher's Clearinghouse 15 years ago and they couldn't find you! You could be a millionaire, he said in a mock Ed McMahon voice.

Claire laughed. You're right, it's probably nothing.

They finished their coffees, touching hands and talking about movies, the holidays, and how life is never as you expect it to be, how it throws you curve balls, but how maybe that's ok because if life was predictable, it would also be dull. Claire commented, I'm ok with where life has taken me, good and bad, because it has gotten me to where I am now—and I'm ok with where I am. No, actually. I am **happy** with where I am. Adam squeezed her hand and smiled. I feel the same way, he said.

When they were leaving, Claire realized that she hadn't seen that little greasy, sad looking mailman in a while.

Chapter 55

Claire and Bob Kimer missed each other and weren't able to talk until after the New Year. Bob Kimer had taken two weeks' vacation, for a cruise with his wife Allyson and their two kids. He didn't forget about trying to get in touch with Claire Cassidy though, and she didn't forget either. Nonetheless, they both had nice holidays.

Claire had seen Adam Friday night and they had spent all of Saturday together. Adam admitted that he felt a little bummed that they couldn't spend Christmas together, but Claire gently shrugged it off. Adam, she said, how long have we been dating, like almost five weeks? Its an awkward time of year to be dating, she said.

Agreed, said Adam. I just feel like . . . he stopped and looked at the ground.

What? Claire said, tilting her head to meet his eyes.

I feel goofy saying this, he said, but I feel like I'm going to miss you.

Claire took a deep breath and looked back at Adam. Yeah, she said, I know. I feel like I'm going to miss you too.

Claire, Adam said, I know this might seem a little early but, I don't want to think that we're dating. I think that dating implies that it's casual, and that we may be seeing other people. This isn't casual to me, and I have no desire to date anyone else.

I'm down with that, Mister, she said, and kissed his cheek lightly. Silly words, but said with an abundance of sincerity.

He smiled. It was late and Claire said, Adam, I should go, you still need to pack, and you have to get up early tomorrow.

Stay, Adam said.

What? Claire replied. But you have to pack, and it's late.

Claire, I mean, stay the night with me. He kissed her, biting her lower lip and sucking it gently. Stay with me, he said into her mouth while he was kissing her. He had his hands around her waist and when a breathless "ok" escaped her lips, his grip strengthened and he replied back "good."

Chapter 56

Adam left on Christmas Eve to see his mom and dad and brothers and nieces and nephews and aunts and uncles and a few cousins as well. Claire thought about how cool it must feel to have family.

She hugged him before she got in her car. Adam, please don't feel weird. I am so happy to be spending time today and tomorrow with my friends. I will have a great holiday and so will you. And I'll be really happy to see you when you get back. When will that be again?

Adam smiled and kissed her mouth, a quick kiss but deep in intensity. I'll be back on Friday afternoon, he said. Can we get together then?

You bet, she said, I'll look forward to it.

She got into her car and Adam stood there watching her start the car. She put down the window and said. Have a merry Christmas, Adam.

He leaned down and said, You too Claire. And next year, I want us to be together for the holidays.

That sounds really nice, she said sincerely, without feeling weird about the implications. Be careful driving, and maybe you could text me when you get there so I know you arrived safely?

You bet, Adam said, lingering near her door.

Ok then, bye Adam.

Bye, sweetheart, he said. He watched her back down the driveway, saw her wave in the rear view mirror, and stood there for a minute looking at the empty road. He sighed and went inside.

Chapter 57

Christmas came and went. Adam enjoyed the time with his family; Claire enjoyed the time with her friends, Bob Kimer and his family enjoyed their cruise, and Albert Palletti's family toasted him at Christmas dinner. He was a good man, Roberta Angellino said about her brother, and she got choked up. Because she realized she had always felt that way, but had never told him.

Adam called Claire from the road on Wednesday afternoon.

How's work, he asked.

It's fine, really quiet, Claire said. I've gotten a lot done but frankly I'm getting a little bored!

Can you take tomorrow or Friday off, he said.

I could, but there's not a lot to do, misunderstanding his question. How is your visit going, are you in the car heading somewhere fun?

I am in the car, he said, but I don't know if I can say that where I'm going is necessarily fun.

Hmm, Claire said, well, where are you going?? I'll let you know if I think it's going to be fun.

Claire, he said, I'm on my way home. Honestly, and please don't be freaked out, I just really wanted to see you, and I didn't want to wait another two days.

Wow, she said quietly, putting her hand to her heart.

I hope that's ok, he said, and I hope that maybe you'll be up for seeing me tonight. Maybe dinner? And I asked if you could take a day off because I thought it would be fun if we could go snowboarding or something.

Claire heard herself say, Oh! Of course, I would love to see you tonight Adam. I'm really happy that you're coming home early.

Phew, he said, I didn't want you to think I was some lame dude that needed to see his girlfriend.

It was the first time that the word "girlfriend" was officially used, and Claire smiled on the opposite end of the phone. She imagined that maybe Adam was smiling too.

And I can totally take a day off for snowboarding, that would be fun, Claire laughed.

That's great, Adam replied, with a bit of relief in his voice. And Claire, he said, about New Year's: I know you want to see your friends, and I have no right asking you so early on, but . . .

Adam, I would love to spend New Year's with you, Claire said. I honestly can't think of a better way to begin the year.

Thanks Claire, said Adam, I feel the same way.

Why don't we do this, Claire continued, we can go to Citrus and meet my friends for a drink, and then we can go back to your house, hang out with the dogs, build a fire, share a bottle of wine, and talk about the meaningful things we learned this year. And maybe the things we look forward to in the new year!

Adam laughed.

Oh, I'm sorry, now I'm the one that sounds lame, Claire said.

No, Adam said, To the contrary. It sounds perfect to me. I'm looking forward to it.

Me too, said Claire.

Should I be nervous about meeting your friends, Adam asked hesitantly.

Not at all, Claire said. I have surrounded myself with warm and loving people. They know that I am very happy knowing you, so you will feel welcomed. Believe me, they will like you, and you will like them. And please, if you want to invite some of your Milford friends, or your colleagues, they are definitely welcome.

Thanks, Claire, he said. I don't really care who else is around, as long as we are together.

Same here, Adam. So I will see you tonight then, Claire said.

Yes, why don't you just come over after you work out, I'll have time to stop at the store, and I can make dinner if that sounds alright to you, Adam said.

Really, Claire said, astonished. More than alright. Are you for real, Adam?

Are you, Claire? He asked in return.

They both hung up with smiles on their faces.

Chapter 58

Claire and Mr. Bob Kimer from the US Postal Service finally spoke on the Tuesday after New Year's. Claire had almost forgotten about him, and the few times that she did remember, she deduced that it wasn't such a big deal; that it had just sounded so bizarre initially but it was probably something really insignificant.

Besides, her head was still reeling from an amazing weekend with Adam. In fact, she had been with him every night since he returned from Rockport.

On Thursday night, Claire and Adam had been discussing 80s music, and Adam mentioned that he had been a closet fan of Adam Ant. With that, Claire looked down and her whole face changed and grew long. Oh no, Adam said, looking sad, almost hurt. What did I say? Do you think I'm a total dork?

And so Claire had the perfect entrée to The Conversation About Douglas, with a heavy sigh and a conversation that began: Well Adam, I have a kind of weird story to share, she said in a tentative tone. She told Adam everything, and in doing so realized that she had never told anyone else *everything* about her and Douglas. Adam sat and held her hand and listened to her story, hearing confusion, ambivalence, sadness, and ultimately, acceptance. When she was done, he hugged her close for a long time. Thank you for telling me that, he whispered in her ear. Thank you for listening and for wanting to know, she said back in a whisper.

She realized that she was really starting to develop some strong feelings for him, and it felt really nice.

Chapter 59

Claire Cassidy? Mr. Kimer asked.

Yes, said Claire.

I'm Bob Kimer, the Postmaster General of Milford. Thank you for returning my call, and please accept my apology for the late reply.

What*ever*, is how Claire wanted to respond, but instead she said, No worries. What can I do for you?

I need to see you in person, Bob said.

That sounds serious, Claire said, with concern in her voice.

It is serious, Ms. Cassidy, Bob replied, But please, you have done nothing wrong, so please don't be worried.

Claire, she said, Please just call me Claire. This sounds so official.

Claire, he said, ok. And it is official. I work for the government. But again, you have done nothing wrong.

Well, I'll be around this evening or tomorrow night, she said, can I meet you somewh—what like, at the post office?

If it's alright with you, I'd like to come to your home, he said.

Um yeah, Claire replied, that's not ok with me, Mr. Kimer, I don't even know who you are. That makes me very uneasy.

Oh, I'm really sorry, Claire. And please, call me Bob. Is there any place near you that you would feel comfortable meeting me then? I just didn't want you to have to drive.

I don't mind driving, Claire said, very confused and very freaked out.

Well, I'm sorry if this seems strange, but I do know where you live, and there's a coffee shop nearby, across from the railroad station. It's called Café Atlantique, are you familiar with it?

Claire laughed inside. Vaguely, she said. I can meet you there, sure. How is 7 tonight?

Tonight is fine, I will be there.

You don't know what I look like too, do you, asked Claire.

No, I don't, and Claire listen, I'm sorry about all of this sounding so official. I just take my job seriously.

I understand, she said, in a way that said she didn't really.

I'll be wearing a bright pink Oxford shirt, he said. It was a Christmas gift, otherwise I wouldn't be caught dead in it. Today was going to be a slow day for me, so I figured I would wear it. Anyway, you can't miss me. Also, I'm very tall.

Claire laughed at his description. He obviously worked for the *post office* section of the government, and not the FBI. Descriptive he was not.

Alright, Claire said. I have long brown hair, I'm average height and I'll be wearing jeans and a black corduroy peacoat. I'll stay up front near the cash register.

Ok, Claire, Bob said. I'll be there at 7, and thank you for agreeing to meet me.

Your welcome, Claire said, and after she hung up the phone she added: I guess.

Chapter 60

Claire arrived at Café Atlantique about 15 minutes before 7, and ordered a large decaf caramel latte with skim milk, no foam. She didn't like ordering that around people, it just felt pretentious to her in some way. Tonight though, she felt as though she deserved a treat. Elena was working and asked about Adam.

Clllllllairrrrrrrrrrrrre, do you have a boyfriend? She teased.

I guess I do, Claire said, smiling. He's a really cool guy, Elena, she said softly.

Oh I know, he used to come in here and read and grade papers, he is such a doll! I haven't seen him in here much lately, except with you.

He's a professor and they're on break right now, so maybe that's why, Claire said in a distracted way.

Who are you waiting for, Elena asked. Is Alex coming tonight?

No, Claire said, I'm waiting for the Postmaster General.

What now, Elena asked, laughingly.

And so Claire explained the story to Elena. As she did, she thought about how kind Adam had been. Do you want me to go with you, he had asked. And Claire almost said Yes, but he had some sort of faculty meeting to discuss next semester's curriculum from 6-9pm and she definitely didn't think this was worth missing something work-related. Instead, Adam planned to stop by Claire's on his way home to hear about the cryptic meeting with the mailman. Postman. Postmaster General.

Claire, maybe you inherited some money from a long lost aunt or something bizarre like that, he had said jokingly. But Claire replied, I can't help but think it's some sort of bill that never got to me, and now there's like insane interest.

Elena, upon hearing the story, had a different take: Ooooh Claire, maybe it's a letter from an old boyfriend, maybe it's some sort of romantic letter that got lost in the mail and it's just now making its way to you! She was almost squealing in delight.

Claire's heart sank, and her brain went into overdrive. Why, in all the imagined scenarios, had she not even thought of something like that, she asked herself.

As she stood there contemplating it, Bob Kimer walked in the door. He stomped his feet to remove the snow from his shoes, and Claire realized why he gave a vague description of himself. She couldn't even see the pink shirt yet, but he was a tall man, an undeniable presence, with light reddish hair and a sincere looking face. When he noticed that Claire was *Claire*, he smiled genuinely, perhaps a bit cautiously, it seemed to Claire, walked over and extended his hand.

Hello there, you must be Claire, he said.

Bob? She asked, even though she didn't need to.

That's me, he said. Should we sit down?

Claire picked up her caramel latte and found a place to sit while Elena made a cup of cardamom cinnamon tea for Bob. He added honey and half&half to it and Claire laughed—partly because she thought it was funny—half&half in tea!—and partly because she was nervous as hell.

I should have had Alex come with me, she thought.

Bob Kimer removed his coat and sat down across from Claire. You're right, she said, that's a very pink shirt. She smiled.

Tell me about it, Bob said, rolling his eyes and laughing at the same time. My wife. She thinks I can "pull it off." Why take the chance, he asked, again, laughing. And Claire politely joined in the somewhat strained laughter.

So, Claire said, expectantly.

Yes, Bob said. Yes. Again, thanks for meeting me tonight, Claire.

Sure thing, Claire replied. I have to be honest, she continued, I am totally beyond freaked out right now.

I understand, Bob said, and Claire noticed that he really did have a kindness in his eyes, but he also seemed a bit apprehensive, and if this was good news, he would have been way more jovial.

Claire, he said, setting his tea down on the small marble table, you know how I asked you if you had lived in Branford years ago?

Yes, Claire replied.

Well, Bob continued slowly, as if he had practiced his lines but forgotten them already. Well, he said again. One of our carriers recently passed away. His name was Albert Palletti. He had worked for the US

Postal Service for over 30 years, mostly in Milford. He was a quiet man, pretty much kept to himself, did his job though. Quite frankly, he wasn't very friendly. I feel bad saying that. He died of a heart attack a few weeks ago, actually just across the street, near the train station.

Claire remembered the greasy looking mailman, to whom she had said, Wait a minute Mr. Postman, and she got a chill. That sad-looking guy who she had always felt strangely connected to. Could it have been him?

Bob was still talking so Claire shook herself back to the conversation, but she talked over the postmaster, asking, Was he a short greasy looking guy? Not to be mean. God, that sounded so mean. I'm sorry.

Bob smiled that "I'm sorry smile." Yes, he replied, that sounds about right. He continued his original train of thought with, His sister called my office after the holidays. She and her daughter went over to clean out Mr. Palletti's house.

Was he a widower, Claire asked vacantly.

No, apparently his wife had left him years ago. He never remarried.

That's why he was bitter, Claire thought. His wife left him and he lived alone, delivering mail for over 30 years. God that sounded depressing. And then he died of a heart attack alone on a street corner. The final scene from Doctor Zhivago flashed through Claire's mind, when Yuri is running toward Lara, and then clutches his chest and collapses.

I'm sorry, Claire said, I didn't hear you, she admitted. Can you say that again?

Bob looked uneasy. Sure, he said. I was just saying that his sister and niece went to his home and found a quantity of mail under his bed.

This is where I come in, Claire said, isn't it?

Yes, Bob said quietly. They sat for a moment without saying a word, but then Bob continued.

From what we can piece together, Mr. Palletti stole certain articles of mail over the years following his divorce. As part of the investigation, we've spoken with psychologists to determine whether there was a pattern with the types of letters he kept. But, we can tell two things: one, he hoarded quite a bit of legal mail. We think there's an association with his wife leaving him for her boss—she was a legal secretary.

That doesn't sound so far-fetched, Claire replied, feeling a little numb. I should have gotten a glass of wine, she thought randomly.

Well, Mrs. Angellino, his sister, explained this to authorities. That's why we think it's reasonable to assume that he was bitter with lawyers in general.

So, was there some sort of legal document I never received? Claire said hopefully, wanting it to be anything but a letter she had wanted and didn't get. Just make it a lame-ass piece of mail, and I can go home and laugh about it with Adam. All that for nothing! she would exclaim.

No, Bob said, looking down at his tea, as if it was incredibly mesmerizing. No, you had a piece of mail that was handwritten and personal—the other kind that Mr. Palletti was holding onto.

She laughed and repeated "holding onto." That's rich, she said. He kept a piece of my mail? She asked to ensure that she was hearing things right.

Yes, Bob replied, this time taking his eyes off his tea and looking at Claire.

And, this letter, it was addressed to me when I lived in Branford, she asked, I mean, that's why you needed to know that I'm the Claire Cassidy that lived in Branford.

Yes, Bob confirmed.

Alright so that was like, 18 years ago or something, she said, sifting through her memories of half a lifetime ago.

It's postmarked, he said quietly. You can check the date.

You have it here? She asked.

Yes, Claire. I'm here to deliver a piece of mail to you that you should have received 18 years ago, Bob said in a serious tone.

Huh, Claire said. This is definitely interesting, she said, trying to be light and funny, but not being very convincing.

Bob said, Claire, I am very sorry that you are just receiving this now, and I don't know how you will react or feel, and that's why I didn't want you to have to drive. I can drive you home if you feel shaken up, it's totally understandable.

Claire felt like she was having an out-of-body experience, like she was watching this scene play out from above. Um, well, why don't you give me the letter and I'll see how I feel, she said simply.

Bob said, Alright, but first, I also need to ask you to keep this quiet right now, while the investigation is still underway. This will be in all the local papers soon, but before we have time to gather all of the facts, I just need to ask you not to speak with the media about this.

Claire laughed at the irony. Her job was to speak with the media, and it was usually Claire that had to give the directive: Please do not speak to the media about this. If you receive any media calls, please contact the Public Affairs Department.

Don't worry, Claire said, I wont speak to the media about this. But can I see the letter?

Bob said, Claire, one more thing. The letter had been opened. When Mrs. Angellino brought it into my office, she had about 40 other letters in a box. The letter was not in its envelope, but we eventually found the envelope in the box. So, I have read the letter. I'm sorry.

Good grief, Claire said out loud without thinking.

I know, I'm sorry. I didn't think there was an envelope and I needed to see if there was a complete name of a sender or recipient so that we could fully investigate.

Ok, Claire said quietly, it's alright Bob. I'm not mad at you, I'm not going to press charges, and I'm not going to the media. Please, just give me the letter.

He reached into his long black coat draped over the back of the chair and from the pocket, pulled out a white business size envelope with letters written in blue ink. It was wrinkled and weathered and as he handed it to Claire, her stomach twisted and a big lump formed in her throat. It was clear, Douglas' all caps, architect-style handwriting. She thought she might get sick but instead just sat there and stared at the characters, and looked at the postmark, yes, 18 years ago, and even though she felt like the world was spinning all around her, she saw the month and day and her brain processed that it was only days after he had left without a trace.

She looked up and noticed Elena looking at her. She thought she had never seen Elena look so serious. This beautiful tall girl with fair skin and long golden-brown hair. She met Elena's gaze and tried to smile but the muscles in her face would have nothing to do with that. She was holding the letter and wasn't sure what to do next.

Bob touched Claire's hand in a kind and not at all creepy sort of way. Claire, would you like to be alone? He asked. Or perhaps I can drive you home and you can read this privately?

No, Claire said, I can walk home, I'll be fine I'm sure. It's from an old boyfriend, she said quietly. Actually, my first real boyfriend, she corrected herself, and then wondered why on earth she would tell this to a stranger.

Have you seen or spoken with him since 1988, he asked.

No, Claire said, He left and didn't say where he was going, and Claire realized that in her hands, the truth about where he went all those years ago was waiting for her.

She wasn't even realizing that Bob already knew what the letter said.

Bob shook his head silently and said, I am so sorry, Claire. This must feel very crazy for you.

Crazy indeed, she replied in a whisper. Wow. She was still holding the letter, just looking at Douglas' handwriting. She used to tease him about how perfect it was. You must have gotten As in penmanship, she would joke.

She stood up abruptly, her chair making a loud noise on the wood floor and startling several people, including herself. She held out her hand. She felt dizzy. It was very nice to meet you, Bob Kimer. Thank you for bringing me this letter. I think I can handle it from here.

Bob hesitated, and she wasn't sure if he had wanted to stay to see her reaction and was disappointed. In fact, Bob hadn't really thought through what this part would look like.

Bob left and Claire walked up to Elena. From behind the counter, Elena looked compassionate and somehow delicate, and Claire said simply, Elena, can I have a glass of wine, whatever red you have by the glass tonight?

Of course you can, Elena said evenly. Did everything go ok?

Well, Claire said, 18 years ago my boyfriend left without telling me where he was going. Picked up and moved and that was that. Apparently though, he did tell me, in a letter, which I failed to receive because some lonely, bitter mailman was hoarding mail, and just so happen to choose this boring looking piece of mail to keep, she said, still holding the letter, not yet having read it.

Whoa, Elena said. Are you ok?

I don't know, Claire said, but the wine might help, she added, trying to be witty. She sat down at a different table, in the corner, and Bob stood outside, looking in at this girl with a glass of wine and a letter in her hand, holding it lightly, looking at it as if it was about to perform a magic trick, and she couldn't take her eyes off of it or she would miss how the trick was actually done.

Bob looked down at his shoes and slowly walked away. Claire placed the letter in front of her and drank her wine. She thought about Douglas, Rick, Jim, Adam, and others in between. She thought about what the letter might say. Did he apologize? Did he go away with someone else? Did it matter? Did he mention Smoky? Did he tell her why he left? She knew her questions could be answered by opening the letter, but she wanted to be calm and have realistic expectations. She wanted to be emotionless, which, of course, wasn't possible. But she wasn't thinking all that clearly.

Claire thought back to fun days with Douglas. She was so young. *They* were so young. Things were much more simple, because they didn't have the experience and wisdom that only come with time. They were young and in love and were happy with the simplest of connections. She wondered what Douglas would be like today, she wondered where he was and she wondered what he looked like. I bet he has a beard, Claire said quietly to her glass of Shiraz, He could pull off a beard.

Halfway through the wine, sitting alone in the corner of a coffee shop that held a lot of memories for her, she turned the letter over and gently peeled back the tape that had been obviously newly placed there, probably by Bob Kimer. Why, she thought, if he told me he had read it . . . but then she seemed to understand as she slid her finger underneath the tape: there is something to be said for being able to open a piece of mail, even if it *has* already been opened. Did that even make sense? Claire thought to herself.

She unfolded the paper, which was unlined, thin, almost air-mail quality, and folded in half. She took a deep breath in when she visualized the stationery tablet that Douglas had used when he was overseas for work. It felt too close and she set the paper down. She took a big gulp of wine and could see words through the thin sheets lying in front of her.

What are you waiting for, it seemed to say, just read me.

It said it in Douglas' voice, so Claire pushed the wine aside and picked up the letter. She unfolded it and again, took a deep breath.

> *Hi hon,*
>
> *I know this is weird, and I can't explain a lot through the mail (government). I need to go away. Everything is fine, so please don't worry. I can't call you, or I would. You know some of the details of my job, but you don't know everything. I just need you to trust me. I want to spend my life with you, Claire. I know we are both young, and I know that in life there are no guarantees. But you make me the happiest man on this earth, and I love our life together.*
>
> *I'll be gone in a few days. I hope this letter reaches you at the right time so you aren't panicked. The timing was not up to me. Pack up some stuff, Claire, not a lot, and meet me at the Bridgeport Ferry on Saturday the 12th at 8pm. It's the last ferry of the night. I'll be on the top deck near the front of the ship. I want you to come away with me and I know it's asking a lot.*

Until I see you, I can't even tell you where "away" is. Even if you don't want to come with me, at least we can say goodbye, and I can tell you why I need to leave. Please don't misinterpret the brevity of this letter as a lack of emotion. I am filled with some sadness about leaving Connecticut, but also with a bit of hope that we can start a new life together, somewhere that is equally beautiful.

I hope you will meet me and we can plan the rest of our lives. If I don't see you, I will understand and respect the fact that you didn't want to leave. I know this is your home, Claire, but you are my heart.

Love always,
Douglas

P.S. Bring Smoky too, ok? He's at the shelter.

Claire read the letter and sat there shaking. She didn't realize she was shaking until Elena came over and said, Claire, are you ok, you're shaking.

Claire looked up at Elena, her big blue eyes full of tears.

Claire, are you ok? Elena said, her voice distressed.

I'm alright, Claire managed to get out. I just, I need to go home, she said.

Do you want me to walk you home, Elena said, I'm concerned about you. What did the letter say?

I'm kind of still trying to process it, Claire said in a far away voice, I'll um, I'll stop back in tomorrow, are you working? I'll stop back in this weekend when I am more composed.

Elena surprised Claire by hugging her tightly. Everything's going to be ok, Claire, she said, I promise.

Claire walked home in the bitter cold and thought about when people say "everything's going to be ok." How do they know? Why do people say such things? And to *promise* that everything would be ok?? Ludicrous! Not to mention impossible.

She couldn't go inside, she just wanted to stay cold, it made her feel alive, it made her concentrate on the air rather than what happened at Café Atlantique between 7 and 9 pm on this first week of the New Year. 18 years, she said aloud, through chattering teeth. 9pm, she thought, Adam should be over soon. Adam, good grief. What will I tell Adam?

She was sitting across the street from her apartment building, on top of one of the picnic benches that overlooked the water. White Christmas lights were still set up, strung all along the harbor, and it looked pretty and peaceful, she thought. She was cold, but she drifted away to another place and time, a fictional place where Claire had received the letter and she and Douglas and Smoky lived together happily, somewhere, she imagined, in the woods. Somewhere along the lines of Little House on the Prairie, only not so extreme. And then she pictured the two of them having children, and watching their kids grow up playfully, Douglas gaining a little weight around his midsection and sporting a full beard, Claire being a hip mom who could always talk with her kids about the latest music. She smiled, paused, and then thought about how young they were, and all that they had yet to learn. Maybe it could have turned out bad, she said quietly, and she watched the breath come out of her mouth. Maybe he could have become a different person—people don't change, Claire said to herself, not fundamentally, but then she was thinking something else, so that her brain couldn't process what her mind was weeding through quickly enough.

Claire? Is that you? She heard a voice from behind her. She wanted to feel startled but instead she just sat there, shivering.

Claire, Oh my God, are you ok, what's going on? It was Adam. He had knocked on her door and when she didn't answer, he called her cell phone, which was on silent, from meeting Bob Kimer, the Postmaster General of Milford. He came downstairs and outside and noticed that her car was in the driveway, so he stood outside in the cold, looking around, trying to figure out where Claire could be. And then he remembered, maybe she's still at the coffee shop, and as he began to walk there, he noticed a girl across the street, under a solitary street light, surrounded by a background of white Christmas lights. Claire, he yelled, is that you?

He approached her and she finally acknowledged that she heard him. Hi Adam, she said softly, almost inaudibly. Claire, you're shivering! Adam said. He sounded very concerned, Claire thought.

What happened tonight, he said, did you meet the Postmaster?

I did, Claire said. She was sitting with her arms folded on her lap, almost as though she was hugging herself. She didn't look at Adam. She unfolded her arms and put her hand out, which was covered by a big, red fluffy wool mitten. On top of her mitten was the letter. It's from Douglas, she said vacantly, Douglas wrote me a letter 18 years ago and I just got it tonight.

Oh Claire, Adam said sadly.

Go ahead, read it, she said. And she looked at him. She thought, Adam is beautiful and kind and genuine. He's a good guy, she said to herself, but before she could continue with her thoughts, she looked around and noticed the snow. Adam, she said, in quiet disbelief, It's snowing out.

I know, Claire, he said, and you're shivering. Come on, let me get you home, you can tell me more inside, ok?

I *am* really cold, Claire said, still rather absently.

I bet you are, sweetie, I bet you are. Come on now, Adam said, and he gently took Claire's arm and guided her off the picnic table. He put his arm around her and walked her across the street to her apartment. They climbed the stairs together and Claire felt as though she had 10 pound weights around each ankle.

Adam took her keys and opened the door, ushering Claire into the living room. Keep your coat on, Claire, he said slowly, I'm going to put the heat on and get this place warm for you. Ok?

Uh-huh, Claire said in a daze.

He came back and watched her from the kitchen. I'm going to make you some tea, so just sit tight, ok?

What's a few minutes for a cup of tea, when I have waited 18 years for a letter from Douglas? She thought to herself.

Chapter 61

Adam sat on the couch next to Claire, who had removed her coat and warmed up a little. She sat drinking her hot peppermint tea, holding the mug firmly with both hands. He was reading the letter and Claire watched him blankly.

Oh my God, Claire, he said, obviously shocked. You mean, some dude stole this from your mail and you're just now getting it, after 18 years?

Yeah, Claire said quietly. Pretty messed up, huh?

Pretty, he said. I'm so sorry, your head must be spinning like a top.

My head *is* spinning, she agreed.

It was Adam's turn to take a deep breath. What do you want to do, Claire, he asked tentatively. Do you want to try to find him?

What? Oh, I don't know, Claire said, exasperated. I think I just want to go to bed, I feel like someone sucked the energy out of me. I'm a wet noodle.

Adam sighed heavily. Of course, he said, I'll go, you get some sleep, and he gave her a sideways hug. I'll call you tomorrow, ok?

Wait, Claire said sadly, Adam, wait. He looked at her. Adam, please stay with me. Don't go, I want you to be here.

Of course I'll stay with you Claire, he said in a comforting tone. I wanted to, but I didn't know if you just wanted to be alone right now.

Quietly Claire said, If there was no you Adam, I would want to be alone. But now that I know you—this isn't coming out right, she said, stopping herself.

I think I understand, he replied. And that's very sweet.

Claire went into her bedroom to change and Adam cleaned up from the tea and called his neighbor. Can you let the dogs out tonight for a quick walk? he asked.

He and Claire went to bed, Claire in her pj's and Adam in his boxers. She turned off the light by her side of the bed and turned to Adam. In the dark she whispered, Adam?—she stopped, and he said, Claire, I'm right here, and I'm not going anywhere. He pulled her close and held her tight. After a few minutes she repositioned herself so that his arm was around her and she was laying with her head on his chest. They fell asleep like that and slept through the night.

Chapter 62

Claire woke up before her alarm went off. She was wrapped up in Adam and she felt warm and comfy. And then as she awoke more, she remembered last night, and the letter, and then she looked over and sure enough, there it was, it hadn't been a dream, there was a Bob Kimer of the Milford Post Office, there was a man named Albert Palletti who stole Claire's letter from Douglas 18 years ago, and there was still a strange lump in her throat. She hated that feeling; when you first wake up and feel ok, and then you remember something that happened the day before, something that wasn't pleasant, and your heart sinks, and you realize that you have to get out of bed but you don't want to.

She looked at Adam and found herself smiling. He looked so handsome and innocent laying there asleep. I really like you a lot, she whispered, you are a wonderful person and I can't wait for us to have more time together. She smiled, turned off the alarm, and snuggled back into him. I'll just be a little late for work today, she thought, and he sleepily embraced her as she made her way towards him.

Chapter 63

Claire finally got up and got ready for work as Adam slept. It was 8am when she walked into her bedroom and woke him. Adam, sweetheart, I have to go to work now, she said in a hushed voice. What, Adam said, seemingly confused. He looked over at the clock. Wow, it's 8?

Yes, she said, just relax, I have to go to work but I made some coffee, and there's skim milk in the fridge. You know I'm a cereal junkie so take your pick, she said, they're all in the cabinet to the right of the fridge.

Wait, Claire, you're going to leave—I don't know, I mean, don't you need to lock the door?

I left a key on the counter for you, she said.

Oh, ok, Adam said, still a little confused.

Adam, Claire said, as she sat down on the bed next to him, thank you for staying with me last night. I really needed to be close to you. I hope that doesn't freak you out. *I hope that doesn't freak you out* had become a common phrase between them, signifying how much they liked each other in such a relatively short period of time. They would say it and laugh, but this time Claire didn't laugh.

He looked up at her and tucked behind her ear the piece of hair that would fall in her eyes. Claire, he said, I know that you learned something very significant last night. I know you are still working through what it all means. I just want you to know that I support you in whatever you think you should do. I want to be the supportive boyfriend, ok? Just be honest to yourself and to me about what you want to do.

What I want to do, Claire asked quizzically. What do you mean?

Well, Adam said, I assume you're thinking about trying to find him.

Oh, Claire said, after a long pause. Well, she said, First let me get to work. We can talk about this later. I'm just, she started—I'm just really happy that you are so understanding. Thank you, that means a lot to me.

Claire, of course, Adam said, and he propped himself on his elbow and gave her a kiss. Claire thought about how nice it would be to snuggle back into bed with Adam, and she told him that. It would be way too easy to slide back into bed with you, she said.

He smiled. I'm glad you feel that way, Claire, he said.

Hey Adam, this letter doesn't change the way I feel about you, she said. It just makes me wonder how my life would have turned out if I had received it. You know, all of our conversations about quantum physics and coincidences and the butterfly effect. It just makes me pay attention to the universe even more today.

I love that about you, Claire, Adam said, looking at her from her bed, as she walked to the bedroom door. And they both noticed the word "love" but pretended not to.

She smiled at him. Have some coffee, she said, take a look at my books, you can borrow any of them, if you'd like.

Thanks, Claire. I'm glad you feel comfortable leaving me here, he said.

I just wish I didn't have to leave, she said. And she turned, grabbed her keys, her water and her bag and looked back at him as she opened the door. Oh, and the key is for you to keep, she said, and shut the door behind her.

Adam smiled and turned in the bed so that he was laying on his side. He looked at the time and then he saw the letter on Claire's nightstand and his smile faded.

Chapter 64

Claire arrived at work around 9:15 and realized that she was late for a meeting that was running until noon. She was happy to realize that something was going to consume her time and she would not be at her desk, contemplating the enormity of the previous evening. Life will never feel the same, she said to herself, and scolded herself for being so dramatic. Really Claire, she said, Get a grip.

After the meeting ended, she walked to Danielle's office. She was trying to figure out the date and remember whether Danielle was traveling. Father Figure by George Michael was stuck in her head and she found it maddening. It was just once that Douglas had said those words to her as they were drifting to sleep one night: *If you are the desert, I'll be the sea; If you ever hunger, hunger for me; whatever you ask for, that's what I'll be.* She still remembered how she felt that in her heart that night.

Danielle was at her desk and not on the phone, and Claire felt an instant sense of relief. She adored Danielle and she laughed to herself that she was really a sap.

Hi! Said Danielle in a welcoming, enthusiastic tone. What's going on Claire, how are things with Adam? She said "Adam" as though she was singing.

Claire said, Do you have a few minutes? I need to sit.

Of course, Danielle said seriously, and noticed that it must be important since Claire was shutting the door, something she rarely did.

Before Claire knew it, the words were pouring out of her mouth. Adam is good. Adam is great. Last night I met a man named Bob Kimer. He's the postmaster general of Milford. He called a few weeks ago but we just connected. He told me he had a piece of my mail, a piece of mail I was supposed to receive 18 years ago. I got it last night. It was from Douglas. He had mailed me a letter asking me to go away with him somewhere. He couldn't tell me in person for some reason, and he didn't explain why in the letter.

Danielle sat quietly with her hands folded neatly in front of her, her face stripped of all color and her mouth slightly open in obvious disbelief.

Claire stopped talking for a moment and looked down at her lap. She quietly said, almost in a whisper, He must have thought that I chose not to meet him, Danielle. How awful.

You have to find him, Claire, Danielle said clearly, slowly, and emphatically.

What, Claire said, looking up with pools of tears in her eyes.

Claire, Danielle said, it's just what you said: he thinks you chose not to be with him. Don't you think he deserves to know the truth? Now that you finally do, it's his turn.

But Adam, Claire began.

Did you tell Adam? Danielle asked.

Of course I did, I told Adam everything, Claire said.

Danielle smiled at Claire and said, Claire, you are incredible. You are so honest and loyal and sensitive to others. Please also think of yourself right now. This guy—Douglas—this event in your young life—it took a huge toll on you. And it shaped who you are, how you approach relationships; your fears, your concerns, your cynicism. And here you are, in front of me, telling me that what you based your adulthood on is inaccurate. This man loved you and you didn't know. That is a horrible shame. An injustice. An incredibly painful fuck-up of the cosmos. I am glad that you finally learned the truth, or at least some of it. But he deserves to know the truth too. Would you have gone with him if you had received the letter?

Absolutely, Claire whispered. I would have gone anywhere to be with him. He was my best friend, Danielle.

And don't you think he should know that, Claire?

I suppose, Claire replied.

What was his last name again? Danielle said in a business-like manner.

Bach, Claire replied, Douglas Ian Bach. Why?

And she saw Danielle swiftly open her internet explorer browser and type in google.com. Wait, Danielle, I don't know . . .

Danielle turned and said, Too late Claire, I found him. That was easy.

Chapter 65

Danielle had googled and subsequently 411-ed Douglas, and cut and pasted his address into an email, which she sent to Claire while Claire still sat in her office.

There, Danielle said, you have his address. You have to think about what you want to do with that information.

Gee, thanks, Danielle. Claire said, I feel like I'm 5.

Danielle looked at Claire kindly and smiled. Claire, you are an amazing person and a wonderful friend. You know I think very highly of you and I only want you to be happy. Carry this around and I guarantee, it will gnaw at you. It won't be fair to you, Douglas, or Adam.

And with the mention of Adam, Claire looked attentively at Danielle. I'm falling in love with him, she said.

I know you are, Danielle said, smiling.

But now this, I mean, what if—

What if is right, Danielle said. You know, you say this to me: the past is the past, but the past shapes us and contributes to who we are. You have the ability to contact Douglas in the present, and set straight the past, so that you can move forward with the future.

Oh Danielle, Claire said, that's good, you should write it down.

And they laughed. Danielle got up and walked around her desk, leaned over and hugged Claire. You are strong, she said, and this doesn't have to be a bad thing. Make it good, Claire. Reach out to someone you cared about and tell him everything you learned last night. And tell him you would have gone with him. Reconnect. Clear the air. Let go.

And Adam? Claire said nervously.

Let me guess, when you told Adam, he was understanding, right?

He was, positively, Claire replied.

Uh-huh. He's a good guy, Claire. Just be open and honest with him as you have been from the start. I think he will be supportive.

He said he would be, Claire said, encouraged.

I believe that, Danielle said.

So do I, Claire said, picturing lovely Adam in her bed as she left for work.

Chapter 66

By 6 pm, Claire had worked her tail off, trying to pay no attention to the time, just focusing on work. She had gotten back to her office around 1, after she spoke with Danielle and ran downstairs to get a salad (which happened to just sit on her desk for the remainder of the afternoon). She accepted that she wasn't hungry, but it was comforting to her to know that there was something there if she needed it.

She looked at her emails. One unread email. It was Danielle's, the one with Douglas' contact information. She hated seeing email that hadn't been opened. What's the harm in opening it, she asked herself? It's not as though opening the email will direct-dial his cell phone. All you will know is where he lives, Claire said to herself. What if he lives in Connecticut? Wouldn't that be weird? No, he would have moved back to Texas, which is where he had grown up. He loved Texas. She closed out of Outlook and shut down her computer. It'll be there for me tomorrow, she figured. Besides, she had gone 18 years not knowing where Douglas lived. She could wait another day. I'm just glad to know he's alive, she said out loud, and she wrapped her scarf around her neck, buttoned up her aqua blue coat, grabbed her bag, and headed out into the cold.

I'm on my way home, Claire said to Adam's voicemail. Will I see you tonight? Let me know. I'll be in the car for about an hour and then I'll be home. I just wanted to connect with you and I thought maybe it would be a nice night to be together. Maybe we could snuggle up and watch a movie. Ok, sorry, I'm rambling. I hope you had a good day. Bye.

Moments later, as Claire was exiting I-84, Adam called sounding sweet and yet insecure. Hi you, he said, how was today?

It was busy, Claire said, and started to tell him about the 9-12 meeting that she was late for, and the random meeting with her boss that went longer than she had expected, which in turn made her rush through slides that she was working on for a presentation—but Adam interrupted her.

Claire, he said, it's not that I don't care about what you're doing at work, I just really care right now about how you are feeling about that news you got last night.

Oh, Claire said, Yeah that letter really threw me, she admitted. I really appreciate that you stayed with me last night. It felt really amazing to be close to you. It was our first night together at my place, you know.

Of course I know that Claire, Adam said, almost as though Claire had insulted him. It was very special to me.

Well, Claire said quietly, I should be in Milford in about 45 minutes. Maybe I could stop by? I'll tell you what I'm thinking about this letter and what I'm thinking about life in general . . . wait, maybe that's more than you bargained for!

Claire, I find your defense mechanism of having to make jokes very endearing, Adam said playfully.

Thanks for calling me out, Adam, Claire laughed.

Adam laughed too, and suggested that Claire go home and change, and come over when she was ready. How about a pizza, Adam asked.

That sounds great, Adam, thanks. I'll eat anything on it except for sausage or pepperoni. Anything else and I'll be fine. I should be there in about an hour, Claire said.

Ok sweetheart, Adam said. And listen, no pressure at all, but if you feel like maybe you'll want to stay, you can bring some clothes with you. I just want you to know that you are welcome.

Thanks, Claire said, I really appreciate that. I'll see you soon, Adam.

And they hung up, or rather, they disconnected, since no one really hangs up phones anymore . . . except for maybe in the office. This is what Claire was thinking about, as she flashed back to the days when she and Douglas would talk on the phone for hours, and neither of them wanted to hang up first. She considered that *they* really *did* have to hang up. How painful that used to be, hanging up. Hitting a button on a cell phone had a lesser effect, she thought. And before she knew it, she was pulling into her driveway. Shoot man, time really evaporates when I think about meaningless things, Claire thought.

Chapter 67

Claire changed into comfy clothes and threw a bag together mindlessly. All she knew was that she wanted to be with Adam right now. She analyzed that perhaps she should lay low and stay home and be alone and think things through some more. But she didn't want to think, she just wanted to be. Isn't that ok, she asked herself rhetorically. Why am I obsessed with doing the right thing all the time, why do I analyze things to such a point where I don't know which end is up? I want to see Adam, he wants to see me, and we can talk about this stuff, I want his opinion, I just need some time to let this sink in. When she had finished packing, she looked around the room and as she was shutting off the bedroom light, the envelope sitting on her night table caught her eye. She looked at it and for a moment stood frozen. And then she gently dropped her bag to the floor, walked around her bed, and sat on the edge of the bed, looking at the letter. She finally very gingerly picked up the letter, as though it might possibly crumble in her hands. She held it close to her chest and began to cry. I am so sorry Douglas, I am so sorry that you didn't know all those years ago: I would have gone with you. I would have gone anywhere with you. I loved you more than anything or anyone. I loved you so much.

Chapter 68

On her way to Adam's house, Claire called Patty Blake and left a message asking for an appointment as soon as possible. She arrived at Adam's about 15 minutes later than she had planned, and she was apologetic. Adam put his hand around her head and kissed her gently. Don't worry, Claire, it's ok, he said softly into her hair. You aren't so late.

She looked at him and smiled. You are so understanding, she said.

Adam smiled back at her. Let's eat, he said, as he took the obviously-overnight bag from Claire's hand. He leaned into her and whispered into her ear: I'm glad you brought this.

Claire made a face that suggested that she felt the same way and said lightheartedly, So what's on our pizza, dear?

Chapter 69

Patty Blake recognized a sense of urgency and uneasiness in Claire's voicemail and squeezed Claire in for an appointment quickly. Claire sat down on Patty Blake's comfortable brown velour couch and unintentionally let out a heavy, exasperated sigh. Patty returned the sigh and said, Oh Claire, did something happen between you and Adam?

Claire's eyes widened and she looked shocked. Oh God no, she replied, and thought *everything is relative*. Shoot, I would feel awful if that was the case, Patty.

But you seem quite overwhelmed Claire, so what is it?

And so Claire told Patty all about Bob Kimer and Albert Palletti and the letter from Douglas in his perfect penmanship.

For the love of God, was Patty Blake's response, which Claire enjoyed because it was so dramatic. But then, upon reflection, Claire realized it was probably warranted.

I know, she responded quietly.

Thus ensued an intense conversation with painstaking detail of recent events. Claire was drained just telling the story, only Patty, like a champion therapist, interspersed all sorts of questions throughout the story. Claire was taken away again in thought, thinking that usually an hour of therapy feels like 20 minutes, whereas this felt more like an entire day.

Patty said that this changed everything for Claire. Claire, she said, do you realize that you have lived your life thinking that you were abandoned . . . and now you have found that you really weren't? She said this as though a new planet had been discovered, full of astonishment.

Claire shrugged and said, But Patty, it doesn't change who I am. I mean, I built my life around a wrong assumption, yes—but I am still that person. How can I change myself after all this time has passed?

Patty smiled. Remember that conversation we once had, Claire, about how everything seems to make sense in retrospect? How right now, things might not make sense, but in time, everything will fall into place, and will give you a reason for why certain things have happened?

Yes, Claire said, but still, can I really change now?

Of course, Patty exclaimed. You have changed even since I've known you. Inherently, you won't change. You are Claire Cassidy, and at your core you will have fundamental traits and qualities that will always be unique to you. At the same time, you are also always learning new things . . . from learning how to snowboard last year, to learning how to trust and have faith in people again. I've watched you do both.

Claire smiled and nodded, looking at the clock and being glad that her time was up. Thanks, Patty, she said. This time has been helpful.

Patty didn't look at the clock, but she said to Claire, I know this is a lot to take in. And I know that when you are ready, you will reach out to Douglas. And I will help in whatever way I can. I'm just glad that you know a truth about something that was sad and mysterious and unsolved for you. When you actually reach out to Douglas, you'll have even more closure. It's ironic, isn't it, since you only recently finished your letter to him?

Claire tilted her head and looked at Patty Blake with a grimace. I'm not sure I like calling it *ironic*, she said. *Annoying* would be more like it.

They both chuckled awkwardly, which made Claire remember to get out her checkbook.

Chapter 70

Claire had decided to wait to open Danielle's email and contact Douglas, until she felt like she could do something with the information she received. She and Adam spent the time in between talking about a lot of things. She told him more about her relationship with Rick, he told her a lot about Amy. On Valentine's Day, he surprised her by taking her to a Rangers games at Madison Square Garden. They hiked with Alobar and Kudra, Claire bought a new car, and they christened it by taking a trip to Rockport to visit Adam's parents, Paul and Janet. The Fosters were kind and warm and genuine, and she felt stupid when she said to his mom that first night they were there, Now I know where Adam got it. But Janet just touched Claire's hand and smiled. They took pictures together of the full moon and the late winter sunsets on the beach. They watched movies, made dinners together, hung out with their friends and walked the dogs. They went snowboarding and they spent several nights lying in bed, talking until the sun came up. They talked about Douglas and talked about what life was like for both of them at 18. They talked about first loves, and they talked about lasting loves. They talked about what it takes to have a successful relationship, and agreed that essentials were commitment, communication, honesty, trust and respect, laughter, intimacy—both physical and emotional, and openness. They shared their feelings, thoughts, desires, and insecurities. They showed each other their chicken pox scars, where they'd had stitches, and played music in the background of just about everything the did together. Claire took care of Adam when he got the flu, making soup and picking up Nyquil. They took the dogs to the vet for shots and burned CDs. They met each others' friends. They got closer every day. Comfortable.

Deep Inside of You was playing loud as Claire prepared a dinner of salmon, couscous and spinach and Adam walked the dogs. When he came in, Adam caught Claire by surprise by saying carefully and slowly, So Claire, when are you going to go see Douglas?

And while it hadn't been in the forefront of her mind during those weeks, it had been in the back of it. And sometimes that's worse. She looked up and at Adam. I guess I should do that soon, huh? She said.

Adam walked around the island counter and put his arms around her. He kissed her forehead and squeezed her tightly. I just think you need to see him, Claire, and see how you feel, he said cautiously.

Claire looked up at Adam, and for a moment wondered in disbelief if he thought that seeing Douglas would actually make Claire want to go to him and be with him. Adam, she started to say, how . . . . and then she stopped, because she wondered herself if she would do this very thing. She couldn't find an answer. She leaned into Adam and let herself be hugged. After a few minutes passed, during which time they allowed the silence to say what they didn't want to say, they drew apart slightly and looked at each other. Claire smiled. I think the world of you, Adam, she said. You have been so supportive and understanding about this situation . . . and others. I know I need to see Douglas. I know I need to do that so that you and I can go forward. I don't want it in the back of my mind, or in the back of yours. Will you come with me?

Adam walked over to the sink as if to wash his hands, but he just stood there. Instead, he looked intently over at Claire and answered, No.

Claire looked back at Adam in shock. No? she asked, obviously hurt.

Adam shook his head. Claire, honey, you need to do this on your own. You don't need me to be there with you. Douglas doesn't need me to be there. I know you can do this, and I will do whatever I can to support you, but I can't go with you. Do what you need to do. Talk with him. Tell him what you learned. Tell him you would have gone all those years ago. He needs to know that. He deserves to know that. Adam's face got long and sad, and his voice got quiet. In a whisper he said, But Claire, come back to me.

Claire felt her tummy sink and she walked to Adam slowly. She interlaced her fingers with his and said softly, simply, You got it, mister.

Chapter 71

A few days later, Claire opened up Danielle's email. It was a bit of a relief to not have that one unread email in bold staring at her. Before she opened it, she closed her eyes and tried to envision where Douglas might be living. She settled on somewhere in Texas, since it just made sense. As she double-clicked on the email, she felt her heart go funny and thought, Shoot, I hope he isn't somewhere like Prague!

He wasn't in Prague.

He wasn't in Texas.

Danielle's email indicated that Douglas was in fact living in Whitefish, Montana. Claire stared for a moment in disbelief: Douglas lived less than 50 miles from Alex's family. She had been there several times. She had even been to Whitefish. It was a beautiful, touristy town. Apparently Julia Roberts had a house there. Richard Gere too. But then, she heard that everywhere she went. She wondered what Douglas did in Whitefish. She wondered if she had driven by his home while she was out there visiting. She shivered. She started to dial his number quickly, realizing that she would chicken out unless she did it quickly. But before she could finish, she hung up. She couldn't do it. And then she analyzed to herself, Well, you *could* do it, you just don't *want* to. She wasn't sure how, but Danielle also had an email address for Douglas: ddbears@gmail.com.

D D Bears, Claire thought. That's interesting. Well, whatever it is, that will have to be my approach. I'm not ready to call him. So he's just gonna have to hear from me in an email.

Claire was shaking as she wrote, her stomach doing back flips:

> *Hi Douglas. I know, weird, huh? It has to be crazy to see my name in your inbox after eighteen years. I'm sorry if it's disconcerting. It feels very weird to me too. I hope that you are*

happy, healthy, and well. You have been on my mind for years
and years—more so recently because of some bizarre events. I
would prefer not to get into it in email. Actually, I would like to
see you. It was so easy to find you. The power of the internet. The
interconnectedness of all things. I remember how you used to say
the world is getting smaller. You were right. In a lot of ways. Would
it be ok if I came out to meet with you? I imagine you have a family
now, and I am not asking for anything other than a conversation.
I think it's long overdue.

Take care,
Claire

She hit send before she could think and analyze it at all. It was 1:33
in the afternoon. At 3:17, she returned from a meeting with the National
Stroke Association and saw an email from ddbears@gmail.com waiting
for her. She felt her stomach grow queasy and read all of her other emails
before clicking on the email from Douglas. She was so afraid of what it
might say, even though she didn't really believe it would be bad. She felt
a gnawing inside and thought about Adam. She wondered how she would
feel if the roles were reversed and she knew she would feel crummy. I hit
the jackpot with Adam, she said to her computer. And then she opened
Douglas' email, which read:

Hi Claire! Wow. It is so nice to hear from you—and what
a surprise! I hope you are happy and well also. I must admit I
am a little concerned about your recent "bizarre events"—I hope
everything is ok. I am well, thanks. I am absolutely up for a
conversation and a visit, if you like. Yes, I am married and I'm
a dad. Being a dad is amazing. Are you a mom? You know I
always said you would be a wonderful mom. I am so glad to
finally hear from you. Tell me when you will be here.

—Doug

P.S. I haven't been called Douglas in ages! Yet I can't imagine
you calling me anything but.

Claire felt strange, as if she was in a tunnel and everything around
her was humming. She wasn't sure of much, but she was certain that she
wanted to tell Adam about this exchange. So she called him and read

everything to him. It made her feel good, it made her feel connected to him—no secrets, no hiding things, despite the obvious opportunity to feel like she wanted to keep it from him; despite the obvious opportunity for him to feel crummy about this reunion of sorts.

Well, Adam said, I'm glad you took this step. How do you feel?

Weird, Claire admitted. Very weird.

So he's married, with kids? Adam asked, and Claire could detect the relief. She couldn't blame him.

Yes, Claire replied. He always wanted to be a dad, so I'm glad for him.

There was an awkward silence. So, Adam said lightly, maybe you should check the flights and see when you can get your hiney out there and tell Douglas about Albert Palletti and how he screwed up your life.

Claire winced. Adam, she said, in an almost scolding tone.

I'm sorry, Claire, he said.

I do not regret where I am, do you hear me, she asked sincerely. I feel like I have some great perspective. I have learned a lot in my years post-Douglas. And I learned a lot about myself when I was with him. I don't regret my life over the last eighteen years. Then she added quietly: and all of my experiences and life-changing events brought me to you.

I'm sorry, sweetheart, Adam said. I am obviously on edge about this. That being said, I am glad you took the initiative to contact Douglas and I know that telling him the story about Albert and the Postmaster will be good for you. I'm even more glad that you are happy to be here with me . . . now.

It will be good for all of us, said Claire, and I am very glad to be with you. I have to get on a conference call but wanted to make sure I told you what happened. I hope that's ok. You are important to me and I wanted you to know.

Of course that's ok, Claire. I am glad you wanted to tell me, Adam said.

Can we talk more over dinner? Claire asked. Though they spent the majority of their time together these days, they still asked about these things on occasion. It meant that they were feeling clingy and needed a little reassurance.

Of course, Adam said. I'll see you tonight at my place?

Chapter 72

Claire looked into flights, as well as getting some time off. She settled on a relatively inexpensive flight from Hartford to Montana via Minneapolis. She had done the trip just a couple of years ago with Alex, to visit her family. It occurred to her that she needed to call Cathy and Lenny to let them know that she'd be in town and ask if she could stay with them. They were like family to Claire, and she thought it would be very comforting to stay with them during this confusing time. Alex had already told Cathy, her mom, about the Douglas situation. Anyone who heard about it was aghast. Claire felt like she should be on Montel or something silly and dramatic. She tried to downplay it, but when she put words around this story, it was kind of dramatic, she agreed.

A Thursday—Sunday trip was therefore planned, but before Claire confirmed with the travel agent, she emailed Douglas to ask if the dates worked for him.

> Dear Douglas,
>
> Thanks for your email the other day and thanks for being open for a visit. I found a decent flight, actually for next weekend. I know that's quick, and I hope that's ok. Anyway, just let me know. I can fly in on Thursday and maybe on Friday we can get together? I'm sure you work, so maybe after you get out of work, or on Saturday?
>
> Claire

She received a reply shortly thereafter:

> Hi Claire, next weekend! Of course. That sounds great, although I have to admit, now I'm getting nervous. I told my

wife, Doreen, about your email. It didn't go over too well. She can be insecure sometimes (like anyone, of course). I think I reassured her enough but I can understand why she feels strange. I'll fill you in more when I see you. Anyway, she told me to ask where you would be staying—you are more than welcome to stay with us. I know, I know, all of it just feels a little nutty. I am really curious about the bizarre events you mentioned. I really hope everything is ok.

Friday will be just fine. I own a store in Whitefish and my employees will be good without me for the day. We can see how things go, but I'm still a relatively early riser. Maybe we can meet up for coffee and take things from there.

And Claire, it's ok. I understand that you weren't ready to make a move like that with me. We were so young. Great times though. Very meaningful time of my life.

—Doug

Claire felt her heart sink and she couldn't swallow. She replied swiftly, typing so fast that she had to keep correcting misspelled words:

Douglas, I have a long story to tell you. I just don't want to get into it in an email. I can understand why your wife is uneasy, and it is very gracious of her to offer for me to stay in your home. I would love to meet her. I am staying with very close friends when I come out. They live in Kalispell. Ironically, I was just in Whitefish a couple of years ago. I wonder if I passed your store. I agree that we had great times. It was a very special time in my life too.

How should I contact you when I get into town?

Claire

Moments later, an email from ddbears appeared in Claire's inbox. It said:

Hi Claire, my store is called DD Bears. Doug and Doreen . . . and bears. I sculpt bears, Doreen is a photographer and shoots bears. That sounds funny. She photographs bears. Why don't you come to the store around 9. There's a coffee shop right around the corner. Crazy that you were out here! It would have been very strange if we had bumped into each other. I guess everything is about timing, huh? It'll be great to see you, Claire. Have a safe trip.

—Doug

Claire confirmed her plans with Douglas via email. She thought about exchanging a phone conversation with him and just hearing his voice in her mind gave her a chill.

Chapter 73

Claire had received a key from Adam a couple of weeks after she gave him a key to her place. They had rationalized that it was a good idea in case Adam was ever tied up at school and the dogs needed to be let out. They were very open with each other but there were times when they both felt that they needed to protect themselves from being so close and opening themselves up for being hurt. Human nature's a bitch sometimes, Claire thought to herself on this subject.

She called Adam and asked if it would be ok if she got to his house before him tonight, that she was planning on leaving work early and wondered if she could get there and start dinner before he got home.

Of course, honey, you have a key for a reason, Adam said.

Good, so you will be home around 6:30ish, Claire asked.

I will, my class ends at 6, Adam replied.

Ok sweetheart, I can't wait to see you, Claire said genuinely.

That's sweet, Adam said happily. I can't wait to see you too.

Claire had determined that work was not the place for her right now. She was distracted and couldn't focus. There were times when work was a welcome way to hide from the things she didn't want to deal with. This was not one of those times. She powered down her computer, grabbed her blackberry, and said goodbye to her colleague and friend Ann, I'm gonna make like a baby and head out, Ann.

Ann laughed. Love that, Claire. Are you ok?

Claire had told Ann about the Douglas situation, but Ann was the only colleague who knew (aside from Danielle, who was first and foremost her friend, and so therefore Claire deduced, not really a colleague). She didn't really want everyone else knowing her business, and she knew that telling one too many people would ensure that the entire company—those who both cared and didn't—would find out the intimate details of Claire's mysterious and devastating first relationship.

Eh, I'm alright, Claire replied. I'm fine. I have a lovely boyfriend that I want to go home and spend some time with. She smiled at Ann as if to say, I'm right, right?

Ann looked at Claire and gave her a knowing smile. Claire, she said, this whole Douglas thing has you in a bit of a tailspin I know, but you and Adam have something really special. I know everything will be ok. Go ahead and see Douglas and see if you can let go and get back to your man.

Claire laughed. I love the way you talk, Ann, she said.

Ha ha, Ann replied. Look who's talking! Now get out of here and enjoy your night.

Claire went home and changed, then to Adam's, stopping at the grocery store first. She decided to make a big fat chicken pot pie, Adam's favorite. She then went and bought three bottles of Cakebread Cabernet Sauvignon—her favorite. She almost literally ran into Isabelle in the Merlot aisle.

OMG, Isabelle, Claire said, delighted and surprised to see her friend.

Oh hi, Claire, Isabelle said, clearly distracted and distraught.

What's up, Claire asked, but before Isabelle could answer, Chris walked up behind her and put his hand on her back, saying, Hey honey, did you want merlot, or cab?

Claire was confused at first. Who is this guy? It wasn't the guy from the gym, and Claire hadn't heard about any new guys, and who would have been around long enough to call Isabelle "honey?"

Claire, Isabelle stammered, This is my friend Chris. Chris, this is Claire.

Claire assessed Chris. He was about 45, salt and pepper hair, more salt than pepper. Tall, at least 6'2" and lithe, like a former basketball player, Claire thought. Nicely dressed in clothes that looked like they were right off a display from Banana Republic: worn but tailored looking jeans, a gray and green cashmere argyle sweater, t-shirt underneath. She looked to see if he was a nail biter or a metro or somewhere in between, and that's when she noticed the gold band.

Oh, Claire said slowly, Hi Chris, nice to meet you.

Isabelle, I'll be up front; Claire, nice to meet you, Chris said hurriedly. Certainly he knew that Claire was a good friend of Isabelle's and that this awkward moment would make a lot of things clear between the two of them.

Isabelle started stammering out excuses and a bunch of stupid, irrelevant things like, We're just friends, I don't want you to think anything is going on, and I know you are sensitive because Rick cheated on you and I didn't tell you we were friends because I didn't want to have to—

Isabelle, Claire broke in and said almost apologetically, I'll call you during the week, ok? To which Isabelle had said without eye contact or emotion, Ok.

Claire waited for them to leave before she paid for her wine; Isabelle turned and looked back when they walked out. Claire looked too and they held a gaze, full of sadness and shame and disappointment. So many things made sense to Claire now: excessive workouts, nights alone, weird explanations for not getting together, and most of all, the completely unjustified low self-esteem Isabelle had. It made her heart heavy.

At Adam's, Claire said a silent prayer of thanks for being in such a wonderful relationship with a man who was honest and trustworthy, and someone who would communicate if there were any issues to discuss. She began preparing dinner by opening the first bottle of wine, and then started making the chicken pot pie and a nice fresh jicama salad. She went into the living room and lit a fire, and returned to the kitchen to make some fresh dark chocolate covered strawberries. She didn't want it to be cliché, this corny dessert, seemingly contrived as the romantic dessert of choice, but she and Adam both loved the combination of dark chocolate and strawberries. Claire was thinking about cheesy honeymoon suites with hot tubs in the shape of hearts and mirrored ceilings when Adam walked in the door.

Hi honey, I'm home, he sang in a goofy, exaggerating way, which made Claire giggle. The wine helped.

Hi dear, she said, as she turned the corner to greet him, and she hugged him tightly before he could take his coat off. She looked up at him and he said, Baby, you needed a hug, huh? To which Claire replied, Actually, I need this. She stared at him for a moment before leaning up and kissing him—at first slowly and lightly, and then still slowly, but deeply. After several minutes passed, Claire leaned back and looked again at Adam. I am so glad you are part of my life, Claire said simply.

Claire, Adam said, and he leaned in so that their foreheads knocked together gently. He kissed her nose softly and whispered, You are amazing. He wanted to say more, but he also wanted to protect himself. He still wondered what would happen in Montana, even though Claire had seemed to be clear that she just needed to see Douglas and tell him about the letter, and tell him that she would have gone with him, if only that postman had delivered her mail. It made Adam shake his head involuntarily, thinking about that what-if scenario. It made him overwhelmed with sadness. By now, Claire was putting the finishing touches on dinner—she had told Adam to "go and get comfy" while she finished up in the kitchen. He took her cue and went upstairs, washed up, and changed into jeans and a t-shirt. He took out his contacts and put on his glasses. When he came downstairs, Claire smiled widely at him and he walked over and hugged her from behind. She turned around and handed him a glass of wine. He took it, and she picked up her own. She raised it to make a toast: to springtime and new beginnings and Persephone. It *was* a beautiful day, Adam agreed, and Claire loved the fact that he understood her reference to the myth of Demeter and Persephone. Claire smiled. To me and you, she said sincerely. To me and you, Claire, Adam replied.

They shared a delicious dinner and afterwards ate chocolate-covered strawberries and laid on the couch together, talking about the meaning of life and happiness and fulfillment and growing old and the passage of time and the joy of letting go and being authentic and honest and raw. They fell asleep on the couch wrapped up in each other.

Claire and Adam eventually went to bed in the early morning hours and continued to sleep wrapped up in each other. They had discussed Claire's trip out to Montana that night as well, and so they spent a little more time sleeping in than usual, since they knew that next weekend, Claire would be thousands of miles away. They both feared this, but for different reasons.

Chapter 74

Claire's flight for Montana left at 3:45pm that Thursday and Adam had classes in the morning and afternoon. She asked if they could meet at the Starbucks on Chapel Street in New Haven in between classes to say goodbye before she left for three days. She was sad about leaving, afraid to see Douglas, terrified of how she might feel, scared that Adam wouldn't want to hang in with her on this, and overall just a bundle of nerves. But she couldn't help wanting to see Adam before she went—she was feeling very clingy.

They had caramel lattes and talked about Adam's last class, which examined the irony of *Romeo and Juliet*. While Adam was in mid-sentence about the Capulets, Claire reached over the table and held onto his forearm. Adam, she said, I am coming back. And I am coming back with the hope that we can continue this amazing relationship that we are sharing. I just want you to know. I don't want to be with Douglas. I want to be with you.

Adam smiled, stood up, and walked to Claire's side. He kneeled down and hugged her tightly. Thanks, babe, he said softly. That's very sweet. Why don't you see what happens out there? I'll be here, that's all you really need to know. I'll be here, waiting for you, if you want to come back to me.

Claire's heart broke. She understood everything. She would feel the same way. But Adam—and she stopped short of saying I Love You, since she was afraid of saying anything which could seem like a last ditch effort. Adam, she continued, You mean so much to me. I love our time together. I value what we have.

I know baby, he kept saying, and by now he just kept repeating, I know, I know, while he held onto her tightly. They stayed locked in an embrace until they both remembered they were in a public place, and then they still needed to be disciplined as they separated. Claire, you love him, just tell him, she said to herself. Adam said the same thing to himself. They both made a deal with themselves that if the other was open and receptive once Claire returned, they would share that. That they loved each other. How simple, and how overwhelmingly complex.

Chapter 75

In all of the years that had passed since she had seen Douglas, Claire would play out in her head the moment when they would meet again. On some level, she knew that they would meet again. Some of her usual visions included: the chance encounter at a grocery store, usually in the produce section, where they would meet and stand frozen for a minute; the airport, where they would both be walking briskly to get to their gates, when they would suddenly recognize each other (this one tended to be dramatic—something about airports); the scenario in which Douglas would find Claire and would come to her office, and she would be on the phone and turn around, only to see Douglas standing in her doorway, and she would have to say distractedly "I'm sorry, I'll have to call you back." As Claire assessed this, she decided that she watched too many movies. She had never considered the present scenario. And yet, here she was, sitting at the airport, thinking about Douglas, thinking about Adam, thinking about life in between. She thought about the relationships she had had and what made them meaningful. Mindlessly, without a clear purpose, she pulled out her notebook and tried to distract herself by doing some work. Instead, she found herself writing: If anything happens to me—please tell Douglas that I would have gone anywhere with him when he was my best friend. Please tell him that someone stole the letter. He will understand. Please tell Adam that I never knew I would experience such a meaningful connection with another person. Tell him I love him, and that I should have told him that before I left.

Claire ripped the page out of her notebook, folded it in half, then in quarters, and then stuffed it between the seats at her departure gate, as she did every so often. If anyone found this after a flight went down, surely they would go public with it. She imagined the note, being plastered all over the internet, on aol, msn, interviews on Good Morning America,

Douglas saying "I had no idea . . ." She didn't picture Adam doing any media interviews. He would shy away and ask to be left alone. She smiled and felt her heart ache, thinking about how kind and genuine and good Adam was. And for a moment, Claire considered walking away from the departure gate. She envisioned herself walking to her car and driving straight to Adam's house and sitting on his porch, waiting for him to get home, she pictured him seeing her as he drove in, looking quizzically at her, until he parked abruptly and ran to her and they hugged and kissed and cried and Claire would say, I just couldn't go, and he would reply, I love you Claire, and he would hold her tightly and she would feel almost like she couldn't breathe, but in a good way. Claire noticed people moving around her and realized that her flight was boarding. Robotically, she got up and stood in line, not even paying attention to the zone she was in. Let them turn me away because I'm trying to board and it's not my zone, she thought, and that will be my sign.

On the plane, she decided that not being turned away was her sign to go. How random, she thought. And then she considered her thoughts on randomness—that nothing is random, and she got annoyed with herself. Claire Cassidy, she said quietly to herself, can you not just take a break from analyzing things? She sighed and looked out the window. It was a cloudy Thursday afternoon in early March, the kind of day when you can smell Spring in the air, you can feel the ground softening beneath your feet, and you can see the buds just waiting to pop on the trees. It always fascinated Claire how that would happen seemingly overnight. She found herself thinking again of the myth of Demeter and Persephone—how Persephone was abducted by Hades, and was destined to live in the underworld for six months a year, having eaten six pomegranate seeds, each seed representing a month of her imprisonment. She pictured Demeter, Persephone's mother and Goddess of Agriculture, roaming the earth despondently each time that Persephone returned to the underworld, abandoning her care for the earth, during which time everything would die, representing the time we call Fall and Winter. And how she would spring back to life, and the earth would follow, when her daughter was returned to her—representing Spring and Summer. Claire thought to herself, Even if that is just a myth, it's such a nicely wrapped up way of explaining the seasons. For all the complexities in life that Claire enjoyed analyzing and deliberating and discussing, she also had a fond place in her heart for the simple answers and the simple stories.

Claire reached into her bag and pulled out her notebook to write, but after about ten minutes of looking at it blankly, she opted instead to reach down again and pull out her iPod. She chose the mix titled "reflective" and decided that she would try to lose herself in someone else's words rather than find herself in her own. As her flight ascended, she leaned back, looked out the window, contemplated what she was about to do, how she was about to feel, and pondered the sadness and beauty of the lyrics to *Love Should*. She closed her eyes and thought of Douglas, but only saw Adam.

Chapter 76

I'm in Minneapolis, sweetheart, she said to Adam.

Hi hon, how are you feeling? Adam replied.

I'm feeling weird and maybe a little uneasy, Claire admitted.

A little uneasy, Adam repeated. It's ok to be scared. I'm scared for you. I'm scared for me too, by the way.

Adam, thank you for being so honest about that, she said. And please don't be scared for you.

Please, Adam said. I am so glad that you and I can be honest about that . . . well, about everything. It makes our connection that much more meaningful.

I know it does, said Claire. I'm very grateful for you.

Hey Claire, call me when you get into Montana tonight, ok? I know you don't want to because it'll be late, but remember, I won't sleep well unless I know you're safe.

Ok, Adam, I will call you in a few hours, Claire said, and she thought of Adam going to bed that night, and finding, when he pulled down the covers, a card and a CD that Claire burned for him, which she titled, simply, I Miss You. Claire was all about themed CDs and this one was, in her opinion, one of the best she had made. Like she would say when she baked, it was Made With Love. She considered the word . . . love . . . and looked out at the sky, a small smile forming across her face, which she could see reflecting back at her in the window.

Chapter 77

Claire finally pulled out her notebook, ready to write. She didn't know exactly what she was going to write, but when she started, it just all made sense:

We grow up listening to fantasies. Our parents read us stories that begin with "once upon a time" and end in "they lived happily ever after." It's a shame, because real life isn't like that. Real life is littered what ambiguity, misunderstandings, drawing together and drawing apart. Real life is about compromise and learning and growing, constantly. Kissing a frog and getting a prince does not necessarily mean that the prince will be good and kind, honest and intellectual. It just means that you will be a princess and you will have prestige. Is that a good thing? Do you suppose that princes and princesses, kings and queens, and other such royalty are happy because of their titles? Is anyone truly happy just because of a title, whether it's King, Queen, VP or CEO? I don't think so. Those things don't define you. Or rather, they shouldn't define you. If they do, chances are you're leading a hollow life.

Because there is so much more to life than what you do for a living. It's about the connections you make along the way. The people in your life who love you, who choose to love you, the people who can walk away whenever they want to, but don't, because you mean something to them. When we're little, we think these connections are easy. You have your parents, you have family, you feel safe. They read you stories about bad situations, evil stepmothers and poisonous apples. You feel desperately sad when you hear these stories, but they turn around and of course the bad people are punished and the good people go on to lead happy, lovely lives. As if it's that easy.

When we're young, we think everything should be easy. People take care of us. We think it's easy to be loved, because it's all we know. As little girls, we envision perfect lives for our older selves. I'm going to meet the man of my dreams; he will be handsome and smart and funny and loving, we think. It doesn't seem unrealistic, it seems certain. In high school, girlfriends tell each other how many kids they will have. My friend Kim said she would have five children. My friend Anne said she wouldn't have any. Kim has no children. Anne has three.

How funny that we think we know. That we can even think we know what we want when we're that young. It's a confusing time for sure, but one thing we always know, no matter what our age: we know that we want someone to love us. That just goes without saying. Who wants to go through life without being loved by a significant other? Who wants to go to bed at night without someone to think of? Someone to hold close, or someone to miss?

The thing is, I thought I knew what I wanted. Someone who was strong and could protect me and make me feel secure. Someone who made me melty. When I was 20, I couldn't have articulated the essential qualities of a partner: friendship, trust, honesty and communication, shared values and morals, the ability to laugh together at the silliest things. Maybe it's because as we get older, we know ourselves better, and therefore know better what we want in a partner. Feeling melty is great, but it can only take you so far. Without true respect, honesty, candor, open communication, love, really, that melty feeling . . . well, melts away . . . and pretty quickly too.

I've learned over the years that a true partner is someone who is not perfect, yet you love them still. No one is perfect. I tried for years to be perfect. I aspired to be everything that someone else was looking for, until suddenly it occurred to me: I wasn't being authentic. And every time I did something that made me feel less authentic, it made me feel like crap. The real me was buried under layers of what someone else wanted. And I just wanted to be me.

And I want my significant other to just be himself. It's not about the hair or the looks or the clothes or the history. It's about being genuine. It's about being honest, which isn't always easy. Just like we were duped by those unrealistic fairy tales we heard when we were younger, we also learned from a young age that lying to spare someone's feelings is acceptable and in fact, generally preferred. Those lies are minor compared to the deeper betrayals that can follow. It's easy to lie. It's the easy way out. And before you know it, you're in your own corner and your partner is somewhere else. If only more people understood the incredible closeness that can be achieved when simple honesty is at the core of a relationship.

Yes, I speak from experience. No, I'm not bitter. I feel enlightened; I feel clear. I feel grateful for having learned these things relatively early in life. My ideal mate is not someone who left without a trace when I was 20 years old. I don't know him anymore. My ideal mate is not the man I married when I was 24. I've finally let go and forgiven myself for being in a relationship that, for too long, caused me a lot of pain. But even still, I learned so much from that relationship. I learned what not to do. I learned what I didn't want. What I couldn't accept. What I needed. I learned about honesty and trust and communication and the hollowness that lives within you when those qualities are missing. I learned about loving a family and I learned about letting go of a family to live authentically. I learned about respecting myself and being true to myself. It wasn't simple. It was accompanied by many tears.

All of these things, though, allowed me to get to a place where I could appreciate someone that had the same values and morals as I do. Someone who values honesty, and not just because he has been burned before. Someone who can stay up all night talking with me, and knows that tomorrow will be tough, but that the conversation and time together was so worth it. Someone who recognizes his shortcomings and isn't afraid to acknowledge them. Someone who appreciates me in spite of my shortcomings. Someone who asks legitimately and sincerely, How was your day? Someone who is guided by truthfulness to himself and to others.

He loves his family and animals. Treats people with kindness and respect. He isn't afraid to have fun and be a total dork sometimes, because he knows he can be himself with me. He holds me when I am scared and I do the same for him. We know that it's not always easy, that relationships—like anything in life—involve effort. But we are committed to each other and feel a connection that goes far beyond the daily minutiae. A strong foundation, a true connection, a willingness to work, and an understanding that things aren't always perfect.

If you have all of these things, no doubt that melty will follow.

Chapter 78

When Claire finished writing, she was well into her flight to Montana, and she had the clarity and peace of mind that had seemed to elude her for years: she was going to let go of Douglas. Finally. And who could say at this point where things would go with Adam? It was ok. Everything was ok. Life isn't something you can map out in your daytimer. For now, things were good and she looked forward to the future, without having to have a timeline or deadlines. And she knew that she adored Adam, that the months they had been together had been full of emotion, intensity, fun, honesty, communication, and downright love. She wasn't worried about whether they would continue to feel this way, she just enjoyed the time they had together, knowing on some level they would always be just fine. She felt lucky and happy and calm.

She pulled out the sheets she had just written and delicately folded them up and placed them between the seat and window. She said a small prayer for the person who would eventually find it: I hope you are open enough to accept some of the truth I have written, she said.

Chapter 79

Claire called Douglas when she got to Cathy and Lenny's. They had picked her up at the airport and hugged and squeezed her as if she was their own daughter. She appreciated their capacity to genuinely show their love. And it instantly made her feel more at ease. Love does that—it gives you a confidence and warmness that cannot be underestimated.

She washed her face and brushed her teeth and put on her comfy pj's. It was a bit colder in Kalispell than it had been in Milford, and she was grateful for the multiple afghans layered across the bed. She wrapped herself in one of them and pulled her cell phone out of her bag.

Hello? Adam said in a sleepy voice.

Hi Sleepyhead, Claire replied.

Hey, are you in Montana? Was your flight ok?

Yup, I'm here and everything's fine, Claire said. Cathy and Lenny picked me up and now I'm getting ready for bed and wanted to say goodnight, and let you know that I got here safely.

Thanks, hon, I'm glad you are there safe and sound, Adam said. So tomorrow's the big day, huh? He asked tentatively.

Tomorrow is the first day of the rest of our lives, she said in her mock Norman Vincent Peale tone, and they both chuckled.

You're a goofball, Claire.

I know, she said. Hey Adam, I imagine that tomorrow will be a pretty crazy day . . . but I am glad to have the opportunity to be here and personally tell Douglas what happened. And I am very glad to have the opportunity to let it go . . . finally.

Me too, Adam said sincerely. Listen, get some rest, and call me tomorrow when you can. I don't have class until the afternoon, so I'll be around when you're on your way to see Douglas, if you want to talk.

If?!?! Claire said. Yes, Adam, I would love to talk with you in the morning. In fact, I can't think of anyone I would prefer to talk with first thing in the morning. Or, for that matter, she said—as she snuggled into the afghan, last thing at night.

And with that, they said their goodnights and both shut their eyes in hopes of getting some—any—rest. Surprisingly, they both slept quite well.

Claire awoke when she heard some ruckus from the kitchen. She opened her eyes and noted the time: 6:30. She breathed in deeply and smelled rich coffee, and remembered how delicious Cathy's coffee was. It made her feel warm inside. It made her think of a coffee commercial. And then she remembered what today was, almost with that feeling of panic, of thinking, can I bail out now? Is it too late? Would it be bad? What if we never connected? Would things really be any different? How do I look? Will Douglas think I look old? Or worse, will he think it but not say it? How will he look? What if he looks better than me? What if Doreen is gorgeous? What if Douglas doesn't give a rat's ass about my story and the Postmaster, and Albert Palletti? What if he gets mad? Or very sad?

Claire heard herself sigh as she put out all these questions to the universe and thought: how exhausting, Claire, and how completely futile! You will learn these things in less than three hours. For now, get your butt downstairs and have some coffee with your second mom.

Chapter 80

Cathy had poured a cup of coffee for Claire before she reached the bottom of the stairs. There's some creamer in the fridge, Cathy said while she stood at the sink.

Thanks, Claire said, I love your yummy coffee, Cathy. I don't need any creamer for it, it's perfect black.

Cathy turned around and said, Good, Claire. And good morning. And with that she gave Claire a huge, tight hug and said, So are you prepared for the day?

Claire shrugged and picked up her mug of coffee, wrapping both hands around it. This will help, she said jokingly. And so will the hug, she said. She winked at Cathy and said, So you wanna see what I'm wearing when I meet the guy who I thought abandoned me 18 years ago?

Cathy cringed, then smiled. You bet I do.

Chapter 81

Claire left for Whitefish in Cathy's 1998 navy blue Ford Mustang, the license plate of which read SugrMountn. It was in homage to her favorite singer (Neil Young of course), and as Claire got in the car she couldn't help but say "bitchin." She laughed and that was a really good thing, because laughing is always good for your soul, she reminded herself.

On her way to Whitefish, Claire connected with Adam and they had a nice conversation about the weather and then about the day ahead. Claire said she was more focused on not getting lost, and Adam said, Yikes, Claire, don't end up in Canada!—a reference to the fact that Claire was really bad with directions. Hey! She said, and they laughed playfully and agreed to talk again after Claire had met with Douglas.

I'll be thinking of you, Adam said, as they said their goodbyes.

I will be thinking of you too, Adam, Claire said. And I already can't wait to see you.

Ok, hon, me too. And as they were hanging up, Adam said, Oh Claire, wait!

What is it, Adam?

Claire honey, thank you so much for the card and the CD. It was so sweet, what you wrote. And I fell asleep listening to the CD. I love that Pete Yorn song. It was so thoughtful of you.

Claire smiled. I think of you, she said. And I didn't want you to forget that I missed you.

Adam took a deep breath. Thanks for reminding me, Claire, he said genuinely.

You got it, she responded. Talk with you in a little while, hon. And . . . thank you for being so supportive.

Chapter 82

It was 8:47 according to the clock in the Mustang when Claire pulled into the center of Whitefish. 837 Main Street was the address of DD Bears, and she was at 1150. So it's on the other side of the road, and it can't be far, she told herself. She passed a coffee shop called Gratitude Café and she deduced that that was where Douglas meant for them to have coffee. She thought about her strong feelings about being grateful for everything in life and she wondered if Douglas felt the same way. This gratitude thing had always been in her, but only in recent years had it become so evident to Claire that gratitude meant everything. It made life richer and it made her kinder. She was thinking these thoughts as she pulled directly in front of DD Bears. She knew to stop before she saw the sign, since there was a massive bear carved out of wood standing as a greeting to all who entered and all who even just walked by. It was beautiful and intricate and for a moment Claire pictured Douglas in a cluttered, dusty woodshop, carving wood into beautiful shapes, listening to Radiohead. Adam Ant just didn't fit, she thought, and that's when the reality of where she was started to sink in. She looked at herself in the rear view mirror and applied some Bonne Bell watermelon chapstick. She looked at herself and shrugged. This is me, she said out loud, and Neil Young, who had been playing in the background, seemed to answer her back. *She's been running half her life . . .*

Claire opened the car door tentatively, slowly, as if she were walking out into a late night, and she didn't want to disturb anyone. She closed the door just as quietly, walked to the door of DD Bears, and studied the bear outside intently while she reached out her hand to the doorknob. She held onto it for a moment, wondering if in a blink of an eye she could wake up and this would all be a dream, but the doorknob turned and confirmed for her that indeed it wasn't a dream.

Chapter 83

Claire stood in the front of the store for less than a minute but it felt more like 10. She stood staring at all of the beautiful photography that was signed Doreen Bach. There were also moose, and geese and mountains and sunsets, in addition to the amazing photos of bears. Claire lost herself thinking, How does she get so close to them? Lost in that thought, she didn't hear Douglas come from the back.

Douglas walked out from the back of the store and saw Claire from behind, admiring the photographs. He felt like the air had been sucked out of his lungs, similar to how Claire had felt when she sat months ago at Café Atlantique with Bob Kimer, Postmaster General, as he explained how a mailman had altered the plans of their lifetimes.

Douglas knew it was Claire because she was the only person he had ever known with hair the color of pure chocolate. He used to call her Claire Cadbury Cassidy, joking that her middle name was not really Catherine, as she led everyone to believe, but that somehow she was a Cadbury descendant and he would eventually trace her ancestry. This was usually when she was on top of him and her hair was falling in his face. He pictured that scene momentarily and his heart broke a little.

She was still lean and fit and her butt still looked great in a pair of jeans. She was wearing black cowboy boots that were worn-in pretty well. She wore a fitted black sweater that he would later learn buttoned down the front with pretty little dark grey buttons in the shape of flowers. She also wore a sweet little silver necklace that you could barely notice until you stood directly in front of her.

Douglas stood there and didn't move. Claire? He said with a tone of knowing, but questioning anyway.

Claire turned without thinking and stood there, facing Douglas, facing her past, her former best friend, her life that never happened, the path she did not follow because she didn't know it was an option.

Douglas, she said, and put her hand to her chest, without considering how dramatic that might look. She smiled and walked toward him, and hugged him without awkwardness. He hugged her back in a way that felt comfortable, in a way that made the years seem to melt away.

Claire felt comfortable hugging Douglas and part of her didn't want to let go. She realized it was the part of her that felt so crummy, thinking that Douglas must have thought she had chosen to stay in Connecticut rather than be with him. She pictured him standing on the ferry feeling terribly alone, and she squeezed him harder at the thought. He responded by squeezing her back and then moving his face back and looking at her. She looked up at him and he said, Good to see you, Cadbury.

Claire smiled and laughed at the reference. Cadbury, she laughed, I haven't heard that name in a long time!

They stood there for a moment just looking at each other and not really knowing what to say. Douglas broke the silence as Claire looked around awkwardly and said, So this is my store, Claire, what do you think? There was enthusiasm and pride in his voice, and Claire couldn't help but detect a sense of wanting approval.

Douglas, she said sincerely, this place is amazing. I was looking at the photographs . . . they're lovely. And do you carve these bears . . . ? They're incredible.

Thanks, Douglas said in a heartfelt way. I do all the carving, yes, and he outstretched his hands, palms facing up. My poor hands have gone to crap, it's nuts. Claire looked and just smiled at him. You were never a hand model, Douglas, she joked.

Douglas laughed too. Thanks a lot! he responded.

Doreen is your wife, Claire said, knowing but needing to confirm anyway, as she looked back at the photographs.

She sure is, Douglas said, For the last nine years.

Claire smiled and looked back at him. Congrats, she said.

Doreen is great, Claire, you would like her. She'll be here this afternoon, if you want to meet her. She's out on a shoot this morning and said she would be happy to meet you if you don't feel too weird. Obviously she feels a little strange and she probably secretly hopes that you are fat and ugly and mean, Douglas said, trying to be light.

Claire looked at him funny.

Sorry Claire, Douglas said. Doreen just had to deal with a lot from me because I really never thought, after you, that anyone had any real staying power. He looked down at the floor and Claire felt that little heartbreak feeling that he had felt only minutes before.

Oh Douglas, she said in a whisper.

No, really Claire, it's alright. Doreen just couldn't understand why you would track me down and contact me after so many years had passed by. I guess I wonder that myself a bit, he said, also in a tone that seemed all at once standoffish and yet painfully vulnerable.

Claire walked over to Douglas and said, Let me see those hands again. He looked at her quizzically and held his hands out obediently. She took them in her own hands, gently interlaced their fingers, and then brought them down to their sides. She looked up at Douglas with tears in her eyes, which she was fighting desperately to keep back. Douglas, she said almost inaudibly, that letter you sent me . . . eighteen years ago . . . it was just delivered in January.

And with that confession, the release overwhelmed her; she blinked hard and big tears rolled down her delicate face. She looked up at Douglas, whose face mirrored hers. He swallowed hard, his eyes blurry from tears. What do you mean, you just got the letter? He asked in disbelief.

Claire sighed. It's a long story, Douglas. Why don't we go get that coffee and I'll tell you everything.

Douglas nodded a small, sad nod and removed his hands from hers. She turned to the door and he placed his hand on her back in a kind, gentle way as they walked out to the street. It made Claire want to cry, but she was already crying, and she searched her memory for a time that she had felt like she wanted to cry but was already crying. This might be a first, she thought to herself.

Chapter 84

By the time they had walked the few blocks to Café Gratitude, Claire had basically composed herself, and Douglas seemed alright. They walked in and immediately Douglas was greeted with a warm welcome. Doug! sang a man behind the counter, how's it going, man? Douglas responded, walking over and shaking the man's hand in that double-handed way, which always seemed very endearing to Claire.

Douglas introduced Claire to Monty, the coffee shop owner and, claimed Douglas, the best barista in town. Monty chuckled and held out his hand to Claire. Pleased to meet you, Claire. As cliché as this sounds, any friend of Doug's is a welcome addition to the family. What can I get you guys?

Claire pondered for a brief moment being in a family with Douglas. Do Douglas and Doreen socialize with Monty and his wife? Do they hang out after the café has closed and drink coffee and talk about the meaning of life? Do their kids play together? Would we have had kids together? How old would they be? She held a mental image of the family that could have been but never was, and it shot her out of her daydream. She noticed Monty and Douglas both staring at her and she looked back at the two of them, smiled, and apologized. I'm very sorry, Claire said, I was totally in another world just now. Douglas smiled and put his arm around her in a way that was loving and supportive—almost brotherly. It's ok, Douglas whispered to Claire. I know this all feels sort of insane. It does for me too.

Claire looked up and smiled at him. Thank you for understanding, Douglas, was what her smile said, without words.

Monty, can we have two large dark roasts, in mugs, please?

Claire spoke quietly, Can you make mine a decaf, she asked.

Douglas looked back at her, his face full of surprise. Decaf?? He asked incredulously.

Claire laughed. I know, she said. About 7 years ago I realized that caffeine makes me sick. Crazy, huh?

Tragic is more like it, Douglas said, laughing.

They got their coffees from Monty, and Douglas pointed to a small bar in the corner. That's where the milk and sugar is, Claire.

Oh, I drink my coffee black . . . now . . . she said, realizing that she had always been a cream and sugar kind of girl until she turned 25, and by then, she no longer knew Douglas. Or, for that matter, where he was, or if he even still *was*.

Boy, Douglas said. This is big news, he joked.

Claire smiled and they sat down. She let out a little sigh. Actually Douglas, it's a little sad to me. All of these years, all of the changes you and I have been through, and we didn't know. All of the subtleties that you know about someone . . . we grew up and into individuals without one another, all because of some stupid mailman. You are now Doug, not Douglas, and I am now Claire who drinks black decaf coffee.

Douglas looked at Claire intently. Yeah, he said, can you please tell me this postman story so I can understand what happened? Why did you just get my letter? And please don't tell me I didn't put enough postage on that envelope. He trailed off, as if speaking more to himself, You know, if anything, I made extra sure there were enough stamps . . .

Claire touched his hand and he came back. Douglas, it's really kind of a crazy story. She looked at him for a moment and thought, He is still so handsome. A little extra weight, which he carries well. The beard, I just knew it. But his eyes, just exactly the same—the same stare, the same kindness, the same beautiful clear gray eyes. The color of slate, she used to say. She sighed again and said, Sorry, I went away again for a minute there.

He shook his head in understanding. So? He asked.

So, Claire repeated. So right around Christmastime I got a call from the Postmaster General of Milford, Connecticut. He left a vague, sort of cryptic message and it took a few weeks for me to connect with him. When I finally did, he asked if I was the Claire Cassidy that had lived in Branford in 1988. I confirmed that I was indeed the one, and he told me in a somber tone that he had an important piece of mail to give me.

Douglas frowned. My letter, he said quietly.

Claire nodded. Yes, Douglas, your letter. Apparently it held some appeal to a mailman who was hoarding mail. He had been doing so for years. He hoarded legal mail because his wife, a legal secretary, had left him for a lawyer in her office. Rich, huh? And they think he hoarded personal looking mail, like the letter you sent me, because he was a bitter man. Nice, right?

Douglas looked at Claire and said numbly, Give me a minute to process this, Claire.

I know, Douglas, I know. She sat quietly for a minute, recognizing that she had had the time to work through what this stinking postman had done, unlike Douglas.

So Claire, he said, Some unhappy dude stole our letter in 1988. You never got that letter. Which means, you must have thought I just took off without telling you. You must have thought I left you . . . abandoned you . . . oh my God Claire, how horrible.

Claire's eyes started to fill up again. Yeah, she said, I thought you left without a trace and just didn't want me to be part of your life anymore. She choked a bit on her words. It was really awful, she said almost inaudibly. And with that, Douglas put his hand on hers.

But Douglas, she said, What about you? For God's sake, you sat on that ferry waiting for me to show up, and I didn't. That must have been awful. Now she was crying.

So was Douglas, as much as a man can in public. His eyes were wet and he was wiping them. Claire, he whispered, I was absolutely crushed.

Claire got up and Douglas got up and they hugged in the middle of this coffee shop in Whitefish, Montana and Claire felt time stand still as she connected with her best friend from what seemed like another lifetime, the person she thought she would spend her life with, the person who at one time had known her better than anyone else in the world. They hugged each other and let themselves be hugged, and when they felt like they had allowed themselves that which they hadn't gotten eighteen years ago, they let go, took a deep breath almost simultaneously, and sat down again, each picking up their coffee cups since neither had words at the moment.

Chapter 85

The coffee is good, Claire eventually said, looking at the mug, and then at Douglas. He chuckled.

It's delicious, he said as if exclaiming the sentiment, obviously in jest.

They laughed. Smiled at each other, kind of in a sad way, and Claire heard herself saying, So hey, tell me about being a dad? How many kids do you have?

Douglas momentarily beamed. I have two, he proclaimed proudly, and Claire felt a smile span her face. Douglas—a dad—I knew it. Interrupting her thought, he said, I have two little girls: Chloe is 7 and Annabelle is 3. They are absolutely the loves of my life, he said.

Well, Claire said smiling widely, pictures???

Douglas pulled out a very thick old wallet, and Claire couldn't help but say, Okay George Constanza! He laughed at the Seinfeld reference and said wistfully, Shoot Claire, we never got to watch Seinfeld together . . . that would have been fun.

There are a lot of things we didn't get to do together, Douglas, Claire said softly. But I am so glad to know that you are happy and healthy, and a dad ! And I am really relieved that you finally know that I didn't choose to be without you. Some miserable old man made that choice for us.

Douglas looked at her, again without words, but obviously deep in thought. BUT, he heard her say, The universe put us back here now. For some reason. Maybe to be able to let go. Maybe to let one another know that it wasn't a choice. I loved you Douglas, deeply, with all of my heart, but cosmic forces were acting against us. Maybe, just maybe, we can make some sense of it because of them, she said, pointing to the photo Douglas had in his hands, of his two beautiful girls. He smiled and held out the picture to Claire.

Claire looked intently at the photo and her heart and tummy simultaneously did little backflips. They were gorgeous little girls, and she said so aloud. Chloe, the oldest, had Douglas' eyes, mouth and nose. Annabelle must have looked more like her mom, a cute little round face and a beaming smile. They look very happy, Douglas.

Oh they are, they're great girls, he said. You know, they'll be home later, with Doreen, if you feel like you're up for meeting my clan. What about you, do you have kids? You must, he said.

Claire shook her head and said, Not yet, but I hope to someday. First I figure I should get married, she said jokingly. Douglas laughed. You will be a great mom, he said sincerely. I can't believe you aren't married though—why hasn't anyone scooped you up?

And with that they delved into deeper conversation. She acknowledged that she had been "scooped up" at one point, but unfortunately by the wrong scooper, and she provided highlights and lowlights of her marriage to Rick. Douglas reacted in a protective way, and said it was a good thing he didn't know the guy, or he'd bash his face in. Claire laughed. With those mitts, she said, he would be in trouble!

They both tried to keep it light here and there but the hours evaporated like minutes as they shared the last eighteen years of their lives. Claire finally learned the reason why Douglas had to leave Connecticut, and Douglas broke down in tears when he heard about Smoky. Eventually composing himself again, Douglas admitted that after Claire didn't show that night, he started having really "low quality relationships" which in essence meant that he slept with whomever was around and didn't make any attachments. I protected myself by not getting close to women, he said simply, with a shrug. There were a couple, but when I felt like I was getting too close, I would bail. It was only Doreen who stuck it out with me and was persistent as hell. She knew I had it in me, I guess.

Claire acknowledged her own fear of being abandoned, and Douglas looked down in a way that seemed ashamed. She touched his chin and he looked up at her. Douglas please, she said, I don't blame you, and I hope you don't blame me, for all of the crap that we have had to deal with because of this asshole mailman that didn't give me your letter. It feels good, after all this time, to know what really happened. I am relieved that you didn't abandon me. I may have lost myself for a while, I may have lost my spirit, and my ability to trust. But slowly I got it back. And today, I feel as though it's back a thousandfold. Don't you, she asked hopefully.

Douglas smiled broadly. Yeah, Claire, that is how I feel. I am really glad that you are ok. I always felt responsible for you, you know, even after I thought you didn't want to come with me. And thanks to Al Gore, he said jokingly, I was able to kinda keep track of you and what you were doing the last several years. It was comforting to know that you had a good job and it just made me feel like you were safe. That helped.

Claire was laughing about the Al Gore reference but as soon as she heard the rest of the sentence, she looked blankly at her empty coffee mug, empty of its second cup at this point. You googled me, she asked.

Of course I did, Douglas replied. You didn't google me?

She smiled a tiny little sad smile and said no. I didn't want to know, she said. I didn't want to know where you were, I didn't want it to be easy to find you, and of course it was very easy to find you when I finally looked.

Why didn't you want to know where I was, Douglas asked with a hint of hurt.

Claire took a deep breath. I didn't want to know you were out there living a life that you chose without me, Claire said simply. I didn't want to think you left without a trace only to now be living in Dallas, working at JP Morgan. It needed to be more complex to me. Do you know what I mean?

Yeah, Douglas said. I think I do. I remember when I first looked you up, and I just kept looking at your name and blinking and thinking, I could call you. Right now. Here's your office number, your email address, shit, even your cell phone number. It was that easy. You were somewhere else, living, breathing, thousands of miles away. Close, and yet far.

Claire responded, I know, it's insane how easy it is to find me. Can you believe they list my cell phone number too? All for a press release about stroke prevention.

Not like stroke prevention is not important, she said quickly.

And Douglas laughed again. Hey Claire, I imagine our whole conversation today can be a weaving together of sadness and happiness. Makes me think of Kahlil Gibran . . . what is that he said about this subject? You used to quote it.

Claire smiled and recited her favorite lines: When you are joyous, look deep into your heart and you shall find it is only that which has given you sorrow that is giving you joy. When you are sorrowful look again in your heart, and you shall see that in truth you are weeping for that which has been your delight.

In essence, you can't know joy until you have known sadness.

In essence, Douglas repeated with a sigh. What do you think Kahlil Gibran would say if he heard our story, Douglas asked.

Claire thought for a moment. I think he would say we truly have the capacity to understand both joy and sorrow.

I suppose we're lucky for that, Douglas said.

Claire nodded. We *are* lucky, Douglas.

Chapter 86

Monty filled their coffees over the hours and put food in front of them even when they hadn't asked for it. He seemed to understand that the exchange was intense, two people who had a lot of catching up to do, and he came and went without them even noticing.

It was only when Claire got up from the table to use the lady's room that she looked over at Monty, and he smiled at her, and she smiled back. Douglas is lucky to have you as a friend, she said without really thinking.

He's a good man, Monty replied.

I know, Claire responded. I knew him a long time ago, she offered. I'm glad to know he has stayed the same good person.

They exchanged smiles and she continued to the ladies room.

When she got back to the table, she said to Douglas, Wow, do you know that it's almost 2 already? We've been talking for hours, she said.

We needed it, Douglas said in mock defense. We deserved it, he added quietly.

You're right, Claire said, thinking, I may never see your face again.

She was thinking of Adam, and what he was doing, and how he must be feeling. When Douglas excused himself to use the men's room, Claire shot Adam a brief text: Hi hon, everything is going fine. I miss you. Be prepared for a big hug when I get home. xo.

Douglas came around the corner and saw Claire smiling.

Whatcha thinking, he sang to her.

Claire said, I just sent a quick text to my BF. Like Doreen, he was a little weirded out about this whole scene . . . but for different reasons, I suppose.

Ah, the BF, Douglas said. That's funny Claire, The BF. You are funny. I miss your sense of humor. But we got sidetracked when you started telling me about him. Tell me about him. And what's different about how he and Doreen feel?

Well, Claire said, He knows that you didn't desert me. Doreen doesn't know that I didn't show up because I didn't get the letter. Big diff, she said, and they both laughed a little laugh, since she sounded like she was a teenager.

Adam knows that I came here to tell you the truth about the letter. He knows the truth. Doreen doesn't. God, Claire said sadly, She must think I'm a horrible person.

She doesn't, Claire, she's not like that, Douglas said calmly. He smiled. You should meet her. She really does want to meet you, and she's probably back at the shop by now. What do you think? Too much? Too weird? I know it sounds strange . . . part of me wants you to meet her because I love her; she is my present and my future. And part of me feels like worlds are colliding . . . that as long as the two of you aren't in a room together . . . he paused, looking down at the floor . . . maybe none of this happened, and maybe you are still my present and future . . . you know, like if you actually got the letter. Silly, right?

Claire reached out and touched Douglas' hand. They really were rough, she thought to herself, like sandpaper. Oh Douglas, she said understandingly, Believe me, I get it. I've had time to let things sink in. But I have imagined hundreds of different endings—and they usually ended with you and I together . . . and very happy.

And with that, Claire pulled the letter out from her bag. Here it is, she said, and placed it on the table. Douglas stared at it, then picked it up and delicately removed the letter from its envelope. He sat and read the letter and his eyes got watery. When he finished reading it, he looked up at Claire and whispered, I'm so sorry.

Claire replied back, Me too.

She said she was going to keep the letter, unless he wanted it, and he shook his head. No, you keep it, I wrote it to you. It's yours.

Claire folded the letter and placed it back in its home neatly. This would make such a good book, she said, trying to be lighthearted.

Douglas looked at Claire and smiled. Well, Cadbury, if you write a book about this, I want some of the royalties.

His phone rang as Claire's phone buzzed. A call from Doreen and a reply text from Adam, respectively. Doreen asked if they were coming to the shop, and Douglas repeated the question out loud to give Claire the option to decide. Claire nodded. She looked at Adam's text that said,

So happy to hear from you—thanks. As for the hug—can't wait. xoxo, Adam.

Claire felt a happiness in her when she saw Adam's text that she hadn't experienced in a long time. She looked up at Douglas and thought, He is on the phone with his wife. Douglas. My former best friend, lover, the man I thought I would grow old with. He is on the phone with his wife. And I am texting the man I love. Yes, she thought, I really do love Adam. Life is so strange, she thought to herself, and was annoyed that the Missing Persons song popped into her head at such a heavy moment.

Douglas hung up with Doreen and looked for a minute at Claire. She looked back and realized what they were sharing was the "last time we're alone" sort of look. She smiled the smile that says "another time, another place". Douglas responded similarly.

Come on, Claire said in way that seemed too upbeat. I'm looking forward to meeting your wife. I want to know how she gets so close to those bears. Douglas laughed. Ok Claire, he said, let's blow this coffee shop . . . but let's walk slowly, ok?

Claire nodded knowingly and stood up, taking her coat off the back of her chair and wrapping it around her. Douglas did the same only he had a heavy, lined flannel shirt. She pictured him wearing it outside his home, cutting wood. They walked over to Monty, where Douglas shook hands again with him, See you soon friend, Douglas said, and Claire waved goodbye, Thank you Monty, it was lovely to meet you, and then they were gone, out on the street, and it had turned chillier, and Claire thought ironically, A coffee would be nice. In all fairness, she was just a little nervous about meeting Doreen. Douglas seemed to sense this and probably tried some reverse psychology on Claire. Or was it deflection?

So Claire, he said, tell me about this BF of yours.

Claire laughed. Adam, she said. That's his name.

Ok, Douglas said, well . . . what's he like?

And so Claire smiled at the thought of Adam and told Douglas about him, how they met that afternoon at Café Atlantique, the fact that they liked the same authors, how they took time getting to know one another, and she paused when she explained how kind he was when she found out about the letter, again touching her hand to her heart without realizing it.

Douglas sighed. I'm glad you had someone there to take care of you, he said, as he put he arm around her shoulder in a way that a brother or very close guy friend would do.

Claire nodded. Me too, she said.

She asked about Doreen and learned that early on, Doreen was incredibly patient with Douglas for all of his commitment issues. She started to feel a warmth and kindness toward Doreen.

They walked and talked and definitely took their time, pausing here and there for the silliest of things "I need to tie my shoe"; "that store looks interesting"; "what's the history behind this statue?"; and so on. But eventually they made it back to DD Bears, and they realized it was probably the last time they would be alone.

Douglas looked at Claire and said, If I haven't already said this, it is really good to see you.

Claire smiled and responded, Same here Douglas. I'm so grateful that we had this time today,

Long overdue, Douglas replied, with a look on his face that seemed to Claire to say *I wish like hell you had gotten that letter*.

And then just like that, Douglas' hand was on the door, and turning the knob and soon they would no longer be in the Douglas and Claire cocoon, they would be exposed to other people, and the word "schmedderlingsraupe" popped into Claire's head, because she had been learning random German words at work, and this one she had a fondness for, for some reason. It meant caterpillar, and she of course associated it with her thought of being thrust out of the safety of their cocoon, and she wondered why her brain took her on so many different twists and turns, when all she really wanted was to be in the present and not acknowledge every little tributary of thought that flitted into her mind.

And then there she was, Doreen, and Claire was jolted back to the present. (Your wish is my command, Claire thought, interestingly.)

Doreen was beautiful, Claire thought, and yet relatively nondescript. Claire would later describe her as the perfect ivory girl—about 5'7", dirty blonde hair, light blue eyes, and a wide, warm smile. But for now, she just held out her hand politely and spoke with Doreen rather absent-mindedly about the photos she had taken and whether or not she had ever been close to being attacked by a bear. Doreen laughed awkwardly, and Claire felt dumb.

With weird timing (though Claire thought, would there ever be good timing?), Douglas interjected into the conversation, Doreen, Claire never got that letter I sent her back in 1988.

Doreen looked shocked, and then she looked hurt. Not for herself, but she looked hurt for Douglas, and even for Claire. That's when Claire's heart fluttered, and she knew Douglas had a wonderful, caring partner. And she was happy.

I'm so sorry, Doreen was saying, but they were all trying to say things to comfort one another and it got awkward in that way until they all stopped and chuckled a little at the strangeness of the situation, everyone there guilty of playing out the what-could-have-been scenarios, mostly thinking selfishly of themselves. Human nature.

Thankfully, the visit wasn't too long, since Doreen needed to leave to pick up Chloe and Annabelle from school. Doreen insisted that Claire stop in for a visit when she was back in Kalispell, this time for dinner perhaps, so that she could also meet the girls.

Claire felt a bit overcome by her kindness and got slightly choked up. Thank you Doreen, she said, I really appreciate that and would love to see you again and meet your family. I did get to see pictures of your girls—they are beautiful.

Thanks, Doreen said, and she walked over to Claire and gave her a brief hug, the kind of hug you share with someone that you have spent some time with, but are only now at the hug-when-I-see-you level. It was a bit awkward, but quick, and very gracious. She also gave Douglas a hug and a familial but not embarrassing kiss on the mouth. I'll see you at home later, Doreen said and smiled, squeezing his hand when she broke from their hug.

Claire smiled and waved as she walked out the door to the store, and again Claire and Douglas were alone.

She's lovely, Claire said.

Thanks, said Douglas. She is an amazing lady. And a great mom.

Claire smiled. So neat that you're a dad, Douglas, she said.

Yeah yeah, Claire, Douglas responded. I feel like an old man! They grow up so quickly. You'll see, when you have children.

Claire smiled wistfully, though she didn't realize it. Douglas walked over, closer to her, and whispered in her ear, Claire, you will be a mom. Trust me.

Okay, she whispered back, and for another moment, time was suspended.

Chapter 87

After more conversation and a tour of DD Bears, Claire and Douglas realized and acknowledged that their time was up. They both let out a little sigh at the same time, and then laughed. Well Cadbury, Douglas said, I guess I should get you to your car, so you can get back to your friends in Kalispell.

Claire nodded and sighed and said, Ooooooooook.

Douglas looked at Claire for a minute, trying to get a question out. Claire could tell, and just stood there in the silence, sensing the unrest in Douglas' voice, understanding the feeling of not wanting to let go, understanding the feeling of when-am-I-going-to-see-you-again-even-though-you-aren't-a-part-of-my-life-anymore?

Just, Douglas said, Just . . . are you glad about the way things worked out?

Ooooph, Claire responded. Douglas, wow, am I glad about how things worked out? Wow. Well, I am glad that we are both healthy, and we are both with people that we care about, who care about us. That's very important and not to be discounted. I like my life, and from what I see, you like yours too. I've thought so many times about Richard Bach books, when he goes to visit himself when he was younger, to tell his younger self certain things. And how he knows that for every decision he makes, there's a split, an alternate path, that in a parallel universe, another version of him is living. I wonder . . . I will probably always wonder . . . what would have been if you and I had been allowed to grow up and grow old together. But . . . Claire's voice trailed off. Douglas waited.

We'll never get to know, she said softly. The universe placed us on alternate paths, and was only recently so kind as to pull us back together. She smiled. I think it's because we both needed to know the truth, and let go of some of the hurt, so we could embrace our futures more clearly and more fully.

And with that, Claire stood with her hands in her coat pockets, looking at Douglas as if looking for acceptance. She felt like Linus in the Charlie Brown Christmas Special, when he recites a passage from the King James Bible —so simple and so lovely that it doesn't merit applause, just a nod of acknowledgement and a moment of silence.

Douglas seemed to smile, sigh, and shrug simultaneously. The universe knows only perfect timing, he said, Or so I hear.

Claire smiled at the reference to the Laws of Attraction, which she and Alex were somewhat obsessed with.

They walked to the car, and it was getting colder, so Claire knew that their goodbye would be brief. They didn't need any awkwardness anyway. Douglas was a married man, and Claire had determined out there in Whitefish, Montana that indeed she loved Adam, all the way back in too-far-away Connecticut. They would share no clandestine or inappropriate kiss, as much as that had the potential of making it perfect for story-telling. They would share an embrace that made up for years of aching for the slightest touch of one another, and it would melt away years of not knowing one another. Physical contact has a tendency of doing that: bringing you back to times and places that are buried under layers of years lived.

They let themselves come undone from the embrace and looked at one another. Without thought, Claire said quickly, yet steadily: Douglas, please let there always be a tiny little piece of you that knows I love you. That'll be why it's okay for me to finally let go. Because I will know that there's a part of you that knows I love you and will always carry you with me. A part of me that will always smile when I think of you. Sometimes sad. Sometimes happy. But always with love.

Douglas smiled in a way that showed he was touched and yet sad, but responded with, You always had a way of finding the right words to articulate difficult feelings, Claire. I'm glad that hasn't changed. And I feel the same way, truly.

Thank you, she said. And she kissed him slowly on the cheek, allowing herself to take in his smell and feel the roughness of his beard. Thank you for meeting me, for allowing me into your life, and for introducing me to Doreen. I am so grateful for our time today . . . so grateful for our time . . . period.

It was a goodbye that was long overdue.

Claire drove away with tears in her eyes, and Douglas watched her drive away, also with tears in his eyes. They both implored the universe for understanding, and they both smiled when their minds turned to Adam and Doreen, and they both felt a calmness, a feeling that all was right with the world, that they hadn't felt in many, many . . . many years.

The drive back to Kalispell was quiet, with Neil Young singing telling Claire that she could be twenty on Sugar Mountain, then telling her about four dead in Ohio, and explaining that every junkie's like a setting sun. She listened to Neil, trying to focus on his words, trying desperately not to analyze the day, just make it back to Cathy and Lenny's without getting lost in thought, or lost on the freeway.

She pulled into the driveway just as Neil was telling her that she was such a woman to him, and she smiled at the thought. Thanks, Neil, she said calmly, I think you're quite nice yourself. She turned off the ignition and jumped out of the car, realizing that right now she just wanted to get home. Back to Milford. Back to Adam. Back to her life.

Cathy was inside playing solitaire at the kitchen counter. Lenny was working third shift so he had just left for work. Claire was supposed to spend the weekend with them, since she was already out there, she had decided to stay the extra couple of days. She also wasn't sure what would happen with Douglas, and had wanted the opportunity to be there just in case things got weird, or they needed more time to discuss things. But here she was, ready to go home, and she bound through the door and ran to Cathy.

Cathy stood up, startled, and said, Well?? What happened? How did it go? Do you need a drink?

Claire laughed. Well, she said, First of all, I need a hug. And she hugged Cathy tightly, and the hug was returned. Claire loved the way this family hugged. Secondly, yes, I will absolutely have a beer, and she opened the door of the fridge to get one. Are you going to join me, she asked. Cathy laughed at the question. Duh, she replied, Of course I will join you! They smiled at each other.

They sat at the kitchen table and drank their beers, Cathy's solitaire game still sitting there patiently to be finished. Claire gave a high level overview to Cathy, feeling that it was only appropriate for Alex to get the complete lowdown first. Cathy listened intently and interjected enthusiasm, laughter, and wistful, sad looks whenever appropriate. It made Claire love her even more. How cool are you, Cathy, she asked. You just let me blab all about this crazy day.

Cathy smiled and shrugged. What can I say, I'm amazing? And they laughed together, until Cathy said, Have you talked with Adam yet?

She hadn't. She had, however, called him when she was back on the freeway and headed back to Kalispell. But she realized that he would have been in class. She had also called Alex, but got her voicemail as well.

I really cannot wait to see Adam, Claire said. I just feel like . . . like I have so much clarity now. Does that seem wrong?

Good Lord, Claire, stop analyzing the shit out of everything, will ya? Cathy asked. Claire would have been hurt had she not heard so much love and care in Cathy's voice. I mean really, she continued, stop being so hard on yourself. You feel like you got some clarity here. It was closure for you. An intense situation. Your life was turned upside down at the beginning of the year, it made you look back on your past, hell, it made you confront your past, face on, here you go, reality in your face, and you know what? It was heartbreaking . . . hearing that your long lost love really never left you after all . . . and then realizing, shit, he must have thought all these years that I didn't want him. Now listen, that kind of crud will get anyone into a strange place. I'm just glad you have Adam, and it's so obvious how much you care about him, Claire.

Cathy, I think I love him, Claire said quietly.

Of course you do, you light up every time you talk about him. I'm glad you figured that out, Claire.

I'm really excited to see him, I just feel like if I could, I would drive there right now. I wish I could blink and be there, Claire said, full of anticipation.

Well, Cathy said, why don't you check flights, I bet you could get there by morning. I can't beam you anywhere, but I can take you to the airport.

But Cathy, we were gonna hang out—

Cathy laughed and got up and hugged Claire from behind as she still sat in her chair. Claire, she said, kissing the top of her head, I love ya. And you can come out to visit anytime at all, you know that. But right now, I think you need to get your ass home and tell this guy how you really feel. Remember, he's thousands of miles away wondering what happened today.

I know, Claire said quietly. She stuck her lower lip out and made a sad look. Cathy looked at her. That'll help, she laughed. Now get up and pack up your stuff. I'll check flights.

And with that, Claire raced up the stairs, knowing that she would see Adam way sooner than she expected, and she just kept thinking about how good it would feel to lose herself in his hug.

Chapter 88

Cathy hightailed it to the airport for Claire to make a direct flight out. It was such a fluke, Cathy said, but Claire laughed and looked around, saying the universe meant for it to be.

Cathy shrugged and said, Whatever, Claire. And then laughed, and so did Claire, and they were hugging and laughing and somehow crying too, the heaviness of the day setting in, the kindness that was being shared, and Claire said out loud, How lucky am I to know you, Cathy?

Cathy wrapped her hands around Claire's head and said, You are very lucky Claire, because my old Ford Mustang got you to the airport in time for this flight. But you really don't have time to tell me how great I am if you want to get on that plane and see your beau.

Claire smiled and hugged Cathy. Thank you so much, Cathy. I love you. Tell Lenny I'm sorry I didn't get a chance to say goodbye or hang out. I know I will see you soon, though.

Love you too, Cathy said, and with that, Claire was off through security and to her gate.

Chapter 89

Claire called Adam from Kalispell International Airport, when she knew she had a few minutes before boarding.

Hey you, she said quietly.

Hi Claire, are you ok?

Yes, she said, I'm fine. It's so good to hear your voice, Adam.

It's good to hear your voice too, Claire.

Adam, I know this whole thing has been weird and uncomfortable, and you have been so supportive, I just want to thank you—

He interrupted her. Claire, he asked hesitantly, how did it go?

Oh, Adam, I'm sorry, everything went ok. It was nice to see Douglas, or Doug, I guess, no one calls him Douglas anymore. He seems happy. I met his wife too. I'm glad I saw him and I'm glad we had a chance to talk. But—she stopped.

But what, honey, he asked.

Adam, I'm leaving tonight, I'm actually at the airport right now.

You're leaving, but you just got there yesterday, he said, confused.

I know, Claire said. Adam, I miss you. She paused. I saw Douglas and I will tell you everything when I get home tomorrow. I do feel very overwhelmed, it was crazy to see him after so many years. But I really missed you, and wished that you were with me. Or wished that we were together. So . . . I decided to make that happen.

Claire, Adam said, in what sounded like relief—

Adam, I just know that I want a future with you, ok? I know that we haven't known each other long and I know that we have a lot to discuss, and a lot to do together, to learn and explore, but I am leaving tonight because I want to see you, I really do miss you and I really do care about you. You make me happy, Adam.

On the other end of the phone, Adam smiled in relief and felt an amazing calm fill his body. Claire, he said, I'm so happy that you're coming home tonight, when will you be in?

I don't remember exactly, Claire said, but it's a direct flight. She laughed. It cost a fortune! But worth it. Why don't I call you when I get home? You'll probably be sleeping when I get into Hartford.

Just call me when you land, he said.

But it'll be early in the morning, Claire said.

I don't care, Adam said quickly. I just want to see you, so call me as soon as you get in.

Alright, I will, said Claire.

Claire, he said, I'm really glad you're coming home.

Coming home, Claire thought, and those two words played back in her head over and over during the course of her flight: *coming home*. She thought about the day with Douglas and she thought about Adam. She thought about her life in between Douglas and Adam, and she wondered about the choices along the way. She thought about how different it had been with Douglas, and yet she heard things in his voice as though he was still the twenty-one year old guy she once loved. She felt good that she had seen him, and she felt good that she was going home to see Adam.

Me too, she said. Now get some sleep, mister. I can't wait to see you.

She hung up and walked to the Starbucks, saying *thank you for coffee*, though I probably had enough today, good grief, though somehow that already feels like it was a week ago. She ordered a decaf vanilla latte from the teenage barista who had jet black hair and a nose ring, tongue ring, and those big earrings that stretch your earlobes out. And when Claire placed her order, the young girl gave her the biggest warm smile, and Claire thought, How dare we ever judge anyone on their appearance?

When she went to pay, she saw the envelope in her bag, that letter from Douglas from eighteen years ago, and she wondered what she would do with it. Keep it where? Why? For how long?

And Claire pulled it out from her bag carefully, and looked at it hard. She looked at the address, she looked at Douglas' beautiful handwriting, she looked at the tape that Bob Kimer had placed over the seal. She felt it in her hands, and heard the announcement that her flight was boarding. She went back to the cute barista girl and asked if she could borrow a pen. The girl smiled and handed Claire a black marker, for writing on cups.

Claire removed the cap and wrote across the front of the envelope: find the people that matter to you. She handed the marker back to the girl behind the counter, and gently laid the letter down at the milk and sugar counter at the airport Starbucks.

Chapter 90

Claire didn't go to baggage because she hadn't checked any luggage. She went straight to her car and got that same sensation she always did when she arrived from a trip, only this time, when she got in the car, she felt strangely comfortable . . . settled. She listened to a Jonatha Brooke mix she had made recently for Adam and thought about the whirlwind trip to Montana. She thought about her past, her future, Douglas, and Adam. When 7am rolled around, she decided it was a civil time to call Adam, so she did. He answered on the first ring.

Claire? he said.

Hi sweetheart, she said.

Where are you, Claire, Adam asked.

I'm on the Merritt Parkway, she responded. I wanted to wait until at least 7 to call you. I should be home in about half an hour.

Claire, can you just come straight here? I'll make you some breakfast and coffee and we can talk. I really want to see you, Adam said.

Really Adam? I mean, I probably look like hell, I've been traveling for quite a while.

Claire, he said, seriously, are you kidding me? I just really want to see you.

I want to see you too, she said quietly. Of course I will come straight over.

Her second call was to Alex. She had been busting, dying to talk with her about everything that had transpired in those last 48 hours. She knew it was early but could not contain herself.

Hi BFF, Claire said quietly, because she thought she was probably waking Alex from a sound sleep. That was not the case.

Hey sister, Alex exclaimed, clearly having been up for a while. What happened, tell me everything!

And Claire did tell her best friend every little detail. She even pulled over to give herself more time to talk, since she didn't want to get to Adam's and have to rush off the phone. It was a good thing too, because Alex had some news of her own.

Claire, Alex said, I am so glad that you saw Douglas. The universe works in strange ways, right? And something interesting happened to me while you were gone . . .

What? Claire said excitedly, did you meet a cute boy or something?

Alex laughed. I always meet cute boys, Claire! And I'm sure I'll meet more of them in New York City.

Huh, Claire said, confused.

I've been recruited to open a new office in New York City, Alex said with excited tension in her voice. My company is paying for a fabulous apartment for me right in Midtown, walking distance from this amazing office space, they're going to pay me a boatload of money, and I'm going to sign a contract to do it for two years. Can you believe it? I said I wanted to live in Manhattan, and now it's happening!

They laughed, and Claire said, Alex, I am so thrilled for you!

Oh and Claire, Alex said as if she had forgotten the best part, There is a Starbucks right next door, are you kidding me?

They giggled and Claire felt warm and happy and good about life. It makes such a difference when the people you care about are happy.

But Alex, two years, right?

Yes Claire, two years. We'll be 90 minutes away. I will still see you all the time and we will always be close.

Always, Claire said, that's true.

Chapter 91

Claire arrived at Adam's around 8am. She pulled into the driveway, walked to the back door, knocked, and walked in.

Adam was standing there waiting for her. He hugged her closely and when they broke away slightly, they looked at each other and kissed softly.

Hi baby, he said, putting his hand through her hair. I missed you. You ok?

I think so, Claire said. I'm good now, anyway.

He hugged her again, then took her hand and led her down the hall to the kitchen, where he handed her a cup of hot, black coffee. Alobar and Kudra greeted her happily.

Thanks, she said, and smiled at him. And hi guys! I'm sure happy to see you both!

He smiled as she played with the dogs.

They sat at the kitchen table and drank their coffees and talked. At first they exchanged small talk about the dogs and the weather, but then Adam put his hand on Claire's hand and squeezed it. Why don't you tell me about Douglas, he said.

Claire pulled apart the honey wheat bagel that was in front of her and sighed. It was really weird to see him, she said softly.

I bet, Adam said, still watching and listening to her intently.

Chapter 92

After breakfast, Claire went home to unpack, work out and take a shower, with the intent of going back to Adam's in the late afternoon. She noticed with delight a wedding invitation in her stack of mail: Lyndsay and Billy. She smiled, thinking about what a perfect pair they were, and looking forward to a springtime wedding.

Adam, in the meantime, took the dogs out for a long walk and worked on the curricula for his upcoming classes. As the sun set, Claire arrived at Adam's with dinner. She said, I hope it's ok, I made some dinner for us, and I brought a bottle of wine.

Wow, Adam said, it smells great, what did you make?

I made some chicken marsala and salad, Claire replied—in my spare time. They laughed.

You didn't need to do that, Adam said.

I wanted to, Claire replied. And I picked up some yummy fresh bread from Scratch Baking, she added.

Adam, she said, as she set the bag down on the kitchen counter, You are so good to me. The fact that you were ok with me going to see Douglas, and that you were so welcoming on my return—Adam interrupted her.

Claire, did this experience not teach you that you are loveable and you are worth the attention and love that you give every day? You are an amazing person, and Douglas knew it even before you were 20. I wish I had known you then, he said with a sigh.

I know, Claire said with a smile, and sat down at the kitchen table. But remember, we find ourselves in places to learn lessons. Douglas actually agreed with me on that one. And the timing was right for me to meet him, Claire said with some finality.

How so, asked Adam.

Well, Claire explained, if I had received that letter at any other time in my life, I wouldn't have been ready for it. Now there's you, this wonderful person in my life, and I was able to meet Douglas and enjoy his company for a day, really it was like taking a stroll in the past—neat, but unsettling because you know it's not real. We spent the day catching up on each other's lives, and it was so great to hear about his life. Of course it was difficult to talk about the letter and the ferry ride that night that I didn't show up, and Smoky, and of course, how things might have turned out differently. But the point is, things did turn out differently—things turned out *this* way. However many parallel universes there may be, this is the one that I am in right now, and this is the one with you in it. And this is where I want to be. With absolute clarity and deep sincerity, Claire said evenly, I really do love you, Adam.

Adam sighed and smiled. He knelt down and rested his arms on Claire's legs. Looking up at her, he replied. I love you too, Claire.

They sat there for a few minutes, looking at each other without exchanging any words. Adam finally stood up and took Claire's hands into his. Let's eat this delicious food you made in your spare time, he said in a whisper.

They sat across from each other and ate, drank wine and talked about Claire's trip. Under the table, their feet were drawn to each other, the desire to feel physically connected, just resting on each other with an occasional tap or nudge to acknowledge that they were still there. Adam listened with intense interest to Claire's detailed account of the day. Claire didn't want to leave anything out and she explained that to Adam. Tell me if I'm boring you with all of the details, she said, but I really want to tell you everything. No secrets, she said.

Adam reached over and squeezed her hand. I love that you want to tell me everything, he said. It makes me feel very connected to you—and I wouldn't want it any other way.

They talked well into the night, until Adam looked at Claire and said, Sweetheart, you need to get some rest. Why don't we go to bed? I'd really like to be close to you right now.

Chapter 93

In the middle of the night, Claire woke up and Adam wasn't beside her, even though they had fallen asleep wrapped up in each other. Claire looked around the bedroom and saw Adam standing at the window, looking out at the full moon. She couldn't see his face, but whispered to him. Adam, is everything ok?

You have no idea, he thought. He had gotten up to look at the beautiful full moon and say a small thank you that his best friend was here with him. And make a promise to a sleeping Claire that he would always take care of her, listen to her, laugh with her, and he nodded his head with a powerful thought: grow old with her.

He got back into bed and snuggled into Claire. Hey, he said quietly, want to go buy some bulbs tomorrow? They won't flower until next spring, but it'll be something we can look forward to.

Claire smiled, her eyes still closed. She felt Adam's warmth against her and allowed herself to be enveloped in his hug. That sounds perfect, she said.

Edwards Brothers,Inc!
Thorofare, NJ 08086
22 March, 2011
BA2011081